VICTORIAN GHOST STORIES

Selected and retold by
Mike Stocks

Illustrated by
Les Edwards and Darrell Warner

Designed by Kathy Ward
Edited by Felicity Brooks

Contents

The Demon Dog

It all started two years ago. I went to stay with my friend Kilmoyle in Ireland. Lily, my wife, was pregnant, and didn't want me to go. I wish I never had.

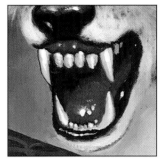

It was at a party in London that I'd bumped into Kilmoyle, and he had immediately invited me over. He was a very grand friend, a lord, the owner of a castle with a huge estate, and I just couldn't resist the prospect of all that fishing and shooting. He also mentioned something about evicting a non-paying tenant from one of his cottages. It sounded like an adventure, and I could hardly remember the last time I'd had one of those.

Lily had a bad feeling about it from the beginning, having heard that Kilmoyle was an intolerant and harsh landlord.

"What have his tenants got to do with you, anyway?" she said. "Let him do his own dirty work."

But all I could think about were the plump fish in Kilmoyle's ponds, and the plumper grouse on his moors, and I wasn't disappointed when I arrived. We spent three whole days fishing and shooting.

On the fourth day we began the eviction. The tenant was an old man. He had lived there most of his life, but hadn't paid a penny of rent in years.

"It's such a paltry sum that frankly, old chap, it's barely worth collecting," Kilmoyle admitted, "but I'm damned if I'm going to have someone make a fool of me."

Our plan was to give the old man twenty-four hours notice to quit or pay. If that didn't work, Kilmoyle explained, we would use "a more direct method".

It was a beautiful stone cottage, small and snug, sitting in the middle of the loveliest valley I'd ever seen. As we came up by the side of the building, I saw the tenant through the window, relaxing by the hearth with a pipe in his mouth and a huge, brown dog at his feet. His weather-beaten face was as dark as teak, and his hair, snow-white, hung down to his shoulders. The room was dirty and in disarray, and it looked like the cottage was in urgent need of repair.

We knocked on the window and banged on the door, and Kilmoyle bellowed a few insults as well, but the old man didn't take the slightest bit of notice. He just sat there, calm and resolute, puffing on his pipe. Eventually Kilmoyle got bored, and thrust the eviction notice under the front door.

"I'll smoke you out like a rat if I have to!" he shouted angrily.

After that we went for a ride and did some more fishing, ending the day with a couple of bottles of champagne at dinner. Perhaps it was the champagne that prompted Kilmoyle to make his offer: he would give me the cottage rent-free for two years, on condition that I organized and paid for the necessary repairs. I accepted immediately. I didn't think it would cost much to make improvements, and, once the baby had arrived, I thought Lily would like nothing better than to spend a couple of summers there.

The next day, feeling slightly the worse for wear because of the champagne, we rode over to the cottage. The old man was sitting in the same chair by the hearth, his pipe clenched between his teeth as before. The dog was nowhere to be seen. Kilmoyle rapped briskly on the window.

"I say, you in there, come out at once! Do you hear me? This is your last warning!"

In answer, the fellow picked up a shotgun at his feet and calmly aimed at us. We threw ourselves to the ground just before he emptied both barrels through the glass.

If I'd been feeling a bit uneasy about smoking this old man out of his cottage, I wasn't any more. We boarded up the other windows, working from the sides in case he fired again, plugged the gaps around the door with mud, and lit a big fire under the broken window. The wind was blowing in just the right direction, and very soon there was thick, acrid smoke billowing into the building.

In his place I wouldn't have lasted five minutes, but he must have been made of sterner stuff, enduring the smoke for nearly half an hour. Just as we were wondering whether we should put the fire out in case the smoke killed him, he kicked the door open and staggered out. He fired wildly at us, missing by a long way, and then collapsed on the ground, black with smoke, coughing uncontrollably. We quickly dragged him away from the house, wrenching the gun from his grip at the same time, and Kilmoyle poured a drop of whiskey down his throat.

Less than an hour later we had put out the fire, emptied the house of its few contents, and boarded it up so that no one else could get in. Kilmoyle offered to take the old man to the nearest village where he was said to have relatives, but he refused this offer, and went staggering off by himself. Feeling satisfied with a job well done, we got ready to go.

Just at that moment we heard a horrible, grief-ridden moan from behind the building.

"Now what?" Kilmoyle said impatiently.

We found the old man standing next to a miserable little pigsty a few yards from the house. A spark from the fire must have

landed on its thatched roof, because the sty had burned to the ground.

"My dog, my dog!" the old man screamed.

It seemed the dog had been tied up inside. Now it was dead. I felt sorry, but it was no one's fault, just bad luck. The crackling noise of the fire, together with the gusty wind, must have drowned out its anguished howlings.

The old man was distraught, moaning and shouting and crying all at the same time.

"I say," Kilmoyle called out, his refined accent sounding rather ridiculous, "I say, I'm sorry about your dog. Of course, you must see that it was an accident."

I felt a sudden stab of pity or

guilt. I was consumed by the desire to help in some way, but couldn't think of how. The dog was dead. No one could bring it back. But perhaps if I had done something – *anything* – or made some gesture of sympathy, then my family would have been spared what happened in the weeks and months that followed.

The old man fell silent, looking up at Kilmoyle where he sat on his magnificent horse. He looked across at me, and to him I probably looked just as high and mighty as Kilmoyle.

He spat on the ground, three times, before launching into a stream of invective. I couldn't understand a word – it must have been in Gaelic – but I knew it wasn't very friendly.

"Come on," Kilmoyle said to me, swinging his horse around.

Together we cantered away.

"What was he saying?" I asked Kilmoyle a little later, when we were trotting to the stables.

"He was cursing."

"Cursing? You mean swearing?"

"No, I mean cursing – laying a curse on us!"

Kilmoyle laughed.

"We're going to be haunted by the spirits of those we've wronged! Our lives will end in terror and misery! Our loved ones will not be spared! The spirits will not rest until they have been avenged!" He smiled as he got down from his horse and gave the reins to a stableboy. "Of course, it's absolute nonsense."

"Oh," I said, "of course."

The following day I received a letter from Lily's sister, telling me to return home at once; Lily wasn't well. Lily's health was poor at the best of times, but to fall ill in the eighth month of her pregnancy was a particularly worrying development. When I told Kilmoyle about it, he immediately offered to drive me to the station in his trap.

We were tearing down the road that led to the nearest town when, taking a sharp corner fairly fast, the horses suddenly swerved, and the wheel on the near side of the trap left the ground.

"Good heavens, we've run over something!"

Kilmoyle reined in the horses and we got out to investigate. It was a dog, a dead dog. It was charred and blackened, so we knew it was the same dog that we had inadvertently killed the day before. Then we saw the old man sitting a little way from the roadside. He was making a strange wailing noise. Kilmoyle yelled at him, wanting to know why he had left the dog's body in the middle of the road, but the old man didn't even notice us. He was too grief-stricken. It was a pathetic sight, but I did nothing to help him. All I could think about was my wife, and after moving the burned carcass from the road, we continued with our journey.

Three weeks later, in England, I became the proud father of a son, called George. Lily recovered quite well after my return, and the birth didn't present any major problems, so the three of us were a very happy little family. But that was before the slow process of tragedy started to unfold.

One evening Lily and I were sitting in the drawing room, chatting and looking at the garden through the open window. The baby was sleeping in another room with the nanny. After a while, Lily fell asleep. I went to my study to write some letters, but I hadn't been there long when I heard Lily screaming. I flung down my pen and ran as fast as I could to the drawing room, where I found her, white as a sheet, clinging to the nanny.

"In the garden," she whispered, pointing outside with a shaking hand. "It's out there!"

"What is?"

She was too frightened to tell me. I told the nanny to look after her, and went out into the garden, but although I searched it thoroughly I didn't find anything. When I went back inside Lily had recovered enough to tell me what she had seen.

She had been lying back in her chair, half dozing, when a heavy pressure on her shoulder woke her up. At the same time she felt a hot, panting breath on her cheek. She jolted upright, crying out, "Who's that, who is it?" She couldn't see anything, but she heard the pit-pat of some animal – "a tiger or a wolf!" – padding across the room to the window. Then she had screamed, and the nanny and I had come running to her aid.

Well, it was my opinion that she had been dreaming. I thought it was one of those vivid dreams that can occur in that semi-conscious stage between sleeping and waking. Lily wouldn't hear of this at first, but the doctor I sent for agreed, saying that it was the only explanation. I put her to bed, and the doctor gave her a sleeping potion. Later, in my study, he suggested that Lily should

have a rest in the country. Her nerves were weak.

"Peace and quiet and lots of fresh air, that's what she needs," he said.

I told him about the cottage in Ireland. I had employed builders to renovate the interior, and they were due to complete the work soon.

"Perfect," he said. "The sooner you can get out there the better."

The situation didn't improve while we waited for the cottage to be ready. Lily was always worried about the baby, forever thinking that something was going to happen to him. I thought this was the perfectly natural anxiety of any new mother, so I'm afraid I didn't take it seriously. Sometimes, if George wasn't with us, Lily started to tremble with fear, convinced that the nanny had left him alone and he was in terrible danger. One night she even woke up *screaming* that something was wrong. I jumped out of bed and rushed up to the nursery. The boy was sleeping soundly.

"Has it gone?" Lily asked me when I got back to our room.

"Has what gone?"

"The dog."

"What dog?"

"The dog that ran up the stairs!" she shrieked.

"Lily," I said, "there's no dog,

"The dog that ran up the stairs!" she shrieked

you must have had a nightmare."

"No!" she shouted angrily.

Why didn't I listen to her? Why didn't I understand that she could see something I couldn't? Every time there was a similar incident, I told her that it was her nerves, or a bad dream, or a shadow on the wall. Instead of listening, I would call the doctor. And rather than take into account her frantic wish to stay where we were, I went ahead with the preparations to move to Ireland, convinced it was the right thing to do.

I wrote to Kilmoyle several times during that period, to let him know my plans and to ask how the cottage was looking. It was odd, but he never replied. When our little household finally arrived in Ireland at the beginning of the summer, we hadn't heard from him.

The cottage looked superb, and I couldn't help congratulating myself for persisting with the move in the face of Lily's opposition. Even she was entranced by its beauty, and we spent a happy hour planning where to put everything. Our baby son, now six months old, gurgled away happily on the nanny's lap, and all in all I felt sure that our luck had turned.

I'd arranged for some local men to come around in the afternoon to carry the furniture into the cottage. They were all rather small, wiry men, but they could carry more with one hand than I could with two. Lily directed them, filling up the rooms one at a time.

Watching them carry a large dresser through the front door, she noticed that they were stepping over the threshold in a curious way. As they approached the door they walked normally enough – as normal as is possible when you're weighed down with a heavy oak dresser – but as soon as they got near the door they seemed to step over something with a long, strange stride.

"Why are they doing that?" Lily whispered to me, pointing at one of the men discreetly.

"I don't know. Ask them."

Lily giggled.

"All right," she said, "I will."

When the men brought in the next piece of furniture, Lily was as good as her word.

"Why are you stepping over the threshold in that funny way?" she said to one of them.

He looked her in the eye briefly, then resumed his work. Lily, exasperated by his lack of response, walked gaily out of the cottage and stood just outside.

"See," she said, "you can do it if you really want to," and she twirled around in front of the door.

Once again, he stayed silent. Lily, embarrassed and frustrated, stamped her foot in a sudden show of petulance.

"Tell me!" she nearly shouted.

The oldest man, a grim-faced, grey-haired fellow of about fifty, stopped his work and looked at her.

His companions did the same. He waited for a few moments.

"It's a grave, Ma'am. The old man buried his dog there."

Then he picked up one end of a wardrobe, and one of the other men picked up the other end, both of them waiting for Lily to move out of the way.

Lily stood stock-still for a few moments, her rosy cheeks blanching, before giving a little whimper and staggering to one side. I rushed to help her, leading her to the back of the cottage, where the nanny was playing with the baby.

"I stamped on the grave," she whispered, distraught, the tears rolling down her face.

"Don't be silly," I whispered back. "It's just a dog."

Lily shook her head.

"Take us away from here, please, take us away!"

The nanny looked on, confused, and the baby began to cry.

"Lily, we've only just arrived! What would it look like if we left on the day we arrived?"

"I don't care! We mustn't stay here, not for a day or an hour or a minute! Why do you never listen to me? Why?"

It's a question I've often asked myself ever since that dreadful day. As usual, I ignored Lily's concerns.

I told her that as soon as the men had gone, we would all sit down and have a cup of tea, to calm down. Then I would go to see Kilmoyle, and she could think about whether she really wanted us to go home. If she still did, then – well, I'd think about it.

"We have to leave straight away!" Lily insisted.

I refused even to answer her. When she saw that I wouldn't be moved, she calmed down a little. I went to Kilmoyle's castle leaving her sitting in a rocking chair with the baby on her knee.

The castle seemed strangely quiet when I arrived. There were no lights in any of the windows, and no servants or gardeners bustling around. I rang the bell. When the door finally opened the butler, still buttoning up his collar, looked surprised.

"Is Lord Kilmoyle at home?" I asked.

"No sir."

"Damn. When do you expect him back?"

The butler hesitated.

"I don't know, sir."

"Today? Next week?"

"I'm afraid I can't say, sir."

"Why on earth not, man?"

The butler shrugged uneasily, as though he wasn't sure what to tell me. I was convinced that there was something odd going on, and I was determined to find out what it was.

"Look here, Reynolds – it is Reynolds, isn't it?"

"Yes sir."

"Well look here, Reynolds," I

repeated, pulling some coins out of my pocket, "Lord Kilmoyle is an old friend of mine. We go back a long way, and I'm sure he'd want me to know when I can expect him back. Perhaps this will jog your memory," I suggested, placing the coins in his hand.

Reynolds looked down at them dubiously.

"That's very kind of you, sir, but I'm afraid it doesn't help, for the simple reason that I don't know when he's expected back." He put the coins back in my own hand, which made me feel very foolish. "You see, sir," he said hesitantly, "there's been a change come over his Lordship these past few months, and he has had to, to *go away*."

The way Reynolds stressed those words – he has had to *go away* – made me shiver inside for some reason. I paused before replying, and then Reynolds suddenly told me what had happened.

"You see, sir, he's lost his wits."

"Lost his wits?" I exploded. "Kilmoyle's one of the sanest, most down-to-earth men I know!"

"Yes sir. Unfortunately he thinks he is being pursued by some sort of, er... demon, sir. As a result, his health has suffered to an alarming extent, requiring his removal to, erm..."

Reynolds coughed discreetly.

"To a what? A hospital?"

"Not exactly sir. An asylum. A lunatic asylum."

There was a silence as we both contemplated this fact.

"Frankly sir, the estate is in total confusion at present, which explains why you were kept waiting so long. Please accept my apologies, sir."

"Yes, Reynolds, yes. Of course."

"Thank you, sir. Good day."

He started to close the door.

"Oh, Reynolds, just one thing before I go."

"Yes sir?"

"This... *demon* – what sort of demon is it supposed to be?"

"I believe it to be a dog, sir."

I mounted my horse and we cantered off. An uneasiness in the pit of my stomach quickly developed into rank fear, and by the time I was in sight of the cottage the horse was galloping at top speed. As I reined in, I could hear Lily's anguished shrieks.

"The *dog!* The *dog!*"

"But ma'am, what dog?" I heard the nanny say, and then I was inside.

"Lily, what is it?"

"Didn't you see? The dog, it came up from the grave, it took my baby! *It took my baby!*"

She started to scream and howl

in grief. I rushed into the nursery with the nanny close on my heels.

"But – I don't understand – he was here just a minute ago," she whispered.

"You didn't see a dog?" I cried, absolutely beside myself with fear.

"No sir, I, I didn't."

I ran out of the nursery, through the rest of the rooms, and then outside, searching for him desperately and hopelessly. All the time Lily was screaming and screaming. I thought about what she had said – "it came up from the grave, it took my baby!"

"Look after her!" I yelled to the nanny, and I grabbed a spade that was lying in the little garden and ran to the front door. Frantically I started to dig.

The old man had dug deep, because the soil started to pile up behind me. Eventually my shovel hit a bundle wrapped in tarpaulin. I quickly cleared away the soil on top of it and lifted it out. I paused. In the background Lily was wailing, and the nanny was doing her best to calm her down. With a heavy heart I unwrapped the tarpaulin. I found... I found the old man's dog, charred and rotting. There was no sign of my son.

I started to feel that there was a small glimmer of hope, that perhaps George had been taken by someone, and that we might find him if we organized a search party. As I shovelled the soil back into the grave, I tried to remember where the nearest police station was.

Then I saw it, there in the soil, dirty and torn but unmistakably his – a torn shred of George's blue blanket.

I sank to my knees, sobbing, and heard, as though it were from someone else, an unbearable wail coming from deep inside me. I felt that my life had finished. My son was dead.

"I felt that my life had finished. My son was dead."

In the two years since our baby was taken away from us, the spirit of the old man's dog has continued its cruel vengeance. Kilmoyle was the first to succumb, haunted day and night until his tortured mind and body couldn't stand it. He's dead.

What do I care about that? Yesterday my wife died in my arms. All this time she has struggled against the curse, sometimes seeing the dog so often that she descended into madness. At other times, though, she seemed to be free of it, and I would begin to hope that we could rebuild our lives. But yesterday morning she saw it again, for the last time. I heard her screaming from the bedroom – *"Keep it away from me, keep it away from me!"* – as if she were being attacked. I ran up to her as fast as I could, finding her almost unconscious. She died soon after.

Well. It's all over now. My friend is dead, my son is dead and my wife is dead. Only I have been spared, though why I don't know. I don't doubt the demon exists, but, for some reason, I've never seen...

What's that? That noise... a scratching noise at the door... No, it's gone, there's nothing... Just a minute... There it is again, that noise, and now... I can hear the sound of something padding across the hall outside.

Something is trying to get in.

A Long Distance Call

We are all going to die. Nothing could be more inevitable, or true. But why do we die, and what happens after? Something happened to me once which gave me an insight into those questions.

It was a tragedy when my friend Vincent's wife died. He was much older than her, and so as well as feeling great grief, he also suffered a sort of baffled surprise that she had died before him. They had married in 1876, when he was forty and she was twenty-five, and had enjoyed over twenty years together. They were very different people, which is perhaps why they got on so well.

Vincent was by no means a weak or passive man, but he could sometimes seem so when compared to Alison. She was boisterous and dominant, though not a tyrant. She loved Vincent very much, and there's no doubt that she made him happy, but there was one thing about Alison which I disliked: her ferocious possessiveness. Despite the fact that he was utterly devoted to her, despite the fact that he was utterly incapable of loving anyone else, she became jealous for the smallest reason.

If Vincent chatted for too long with a female acquaintance, Alison would march up to him and whisk him off. It was unnecessary and rude, but I suppose most marriages have their peculiarities, and this was theirs.

It was Vincent's nature just to put up with the way she behaved, but the consequence was that they eventually offended nearly everyone they knew, and as the years passed they became more and more isolated and dependent on each other. When Alison died at the age of forty-nine after an illness lasting about two months, Vincent had few friends left. Perhaps the only reason that he was still in contact with me was that I hadn't married, so there was no partner who Alison could offend. Even I hadn't seen him for some years, and didn't regard myself as a close friend any more.

I was surprised – embarrassed, even – when, after the funeral, he asked me to stay with him for a while. The idea didn't appeal to me. And was I really the only friend he could muster? However, I felt that I had little choice but to agree. Someone had to keep him company, at least for a few days, and yet it almost seemed to stress how alone he was without his wife.

He lived way out in the country, in a tiny village called Ellerdon. I loathe the country. Whenever I go there, people always want me to kill animals. They expect me to get on a horse and chase a fox across three counties until it drops dead, or shoot a perfectly healthy duck out of the sky. There's no doubt in my mind that the country is a very strange place indeed, and that the people who live there are even stranger. I couldn't refuse Vincent's request to stay with him, but I anticipated a very dull time. In fact I couldn't help feeling more sorry for myself than I was feeling for him.

The evening after the funeral was incredibly gloomy, as you would expect. Vincent and I sat together in his library. There wasn't much to say. His wife was dead. He had loved her, and now he had to live without her. My presence seemed to help him a little. I read the paper, and he pretended to read a book, although I knew his thoughts were far away. A grandfather clock ticked the time away loudly.

After an hour or two Jenkins entered the room. Jenkins had been Vincent's servant for more years than either of them could remember. There was something oddly soothing in the way he plodded slowly across the library to us.

"A glass of port, sir?"

"Thank you Jenkins, yes."

Watching him pour the port, I couldn't help thinking that, now Alison was dead, Jenkins was almost certainly the most important person in Vincent's life.

"I thought I might ride with the hunt tomorrow," Vincent said, not aware how much this made my heart sink. "It'll help me keep my mind off Alison. Why don't you come too? It must be ages since you rode."

"I don't enjoy it, Vincent. It's a bit gory for me".

"Nonsense. Most of the time we never get near a fox. And you're an excellent horseman."

"I'm sorry Vincent, but I really dislike riding and I absolutely can't stand fox hunting."

It was at this point that the phone rang.

Now, there is nothing unusual about a ringing telephone. I was vaguely surprised that Vincent *had* a telephone, but apart from that I could see nothing surprising or frightening about it ringing. I say this because, as soon it started, Vincent jumped up from his chair with a strange, yelping noise. It was rather like the amazed squeal of a newly injured animal.

The telephone continued to ring. I looked at Vincent. His face was nearly white, and his eyes were bulging out of his head as he stared, unblinking, at the telephone. I don't know how long we remained like this, with me staring at Vincent and Vincent staring at the telephone. It was long enough for the device to stop ringing. After a few moments, Vincent sank back down in his chair.

I wasn't sure what to say. Clearly his grief had left him in an unstable condition.

"Sudden noises can be very startling," I murmured eventually, conscious that it was a pointless thing to say, but that something had to be said.

Vincent didn't answer.

"I didn't know that you could get telephones this far out in the country," I continued.

"I had it put in when Alison fell ill," Vincent said eventually. "It links her sickroom with the library. If I was down here and she wanted me, then she could just ring."

"Yes," I said sympathetically. "I can see why you were so startled now. It must have been... well, quite a painful reminder."

Once again, Vincent fell silent.

"Who was ringing you, do you think?" I asked. "Obviously it was one of the servants, but I can't think which one it would be. I mean, as well as being thoughtless, it's just not right for a servant to ring you up! You'll have to have a word with them."

"It wasn't one of the servants," he answered.

"Oh? Who was it then?"

He walked over to the phone, picked it up, and held it out in front of me. The wire hung down limply.

"I disconnected it when she died," he said in a strange, flat voice.

I felt an uncomfortable sensation creep over me, along my arms and legs and up the back of my neck. Though consciously remaining in control of my outward gestures and expressions, my heart was pounding a rapid and irregular beat.

"These things can generally be... explained," I suggested.

"Can they?"

"Of course."

"How?"

"Oh, you know."

Vincent looked at me, almost angrily.

"No," he said, "no, I do not know."

"A tasteless trick, or—"

"But the damn thing isn't even connected!" he said emphatically, swinging the wire from left to right.

"It could be an electrical storm in the air," I said feebly, "producing some sort of – bizarre effect. Maybe it's something like that which has..."

My voice tailed away. Vincent was looking at me, perhaps with some justification, as if I were a complete idiot. The telephone started to ring again. It was chilling. There was something even more terrible about it this time – he was still holding it.

For a few moments he gazed at the telephone with helpless horror, as if it were a venomous snake. I clutched my chair. Perhaps I even gasped. As for Vincent, he gave the same yelp of fear and shock as before, slamming the instrument down on the desk and stepping away from it. I could see the wire draped across the desk and hanging over the edge. The ringing continued.

"Are you going to answer it?" I managed to whisper eventually.

"No, I am not."

"Well I am."

I reached across cautiously and put my hand on the receiver, my fingers closing slowly around it. My courage failed slightly when I felt the vibrations produced by the ringing, as I'd been hoping that the sound was coming from elsewhere, that someone was playing a sick joke.

"Hello?"

There was a crackling, hissing noise, followed by a voice. It was faint and distant, but utterly unmistakable. It was Alison.

He gave the same yelp of fear and shock as before...

"Tell my husband I'm expecting him tomorrow."

I waited for her to say something else or for the line to go dead. Neither happened. The hissing and crackling continued, as though the connection were to a place far away.

"Hello?" I said loudly, then, when there was no reply, I put down the receiver and turned to Vincent.

"No one there," I said.

At six o'clock the following morning, when Vincent came down wearing the scarlet coat of the Ellerdon Hunt, I was already up. He looked as though his night had been as troubled as mine. We exchanged greetings, but neither of us said anything about the previous night. He was amazed to see me up so early.

"Instead of going on the hunt," I said during breakfast, as casually as I could, "I was wondering if you'd like to go on a long walk with me."

"A long walk?"

"Yes."

"With you? I thought you didn't like walking?"

"Yes, er... I just thought it might do you good."

He looked at me curiously.

"Well, it's very nice of you to suggest it. How about tomorrow? You see, the thing is, we can go on a walk any time we like, but there isn't another hunt for three weeks."

"No," I said slowly, "I suppose not. Do you think I could... Is it too late to... Can I come on the hunt too?"

Vincent eyed me strangely.

"If you like."

I stuck to him like a leech that day. Wherever he went, I was there, trying to anticipate and prevent the accident which I was sure was going to happen. I attempted, whenever I could, to jump the hedges and the fences first, often shouting warnings over my shoulder about what was on the other side. He didn't exactly appreciate this advice.

Once I headed him off from jumping a gate. It wasn't high, and the ground was firm, but it gave me a bad feeling as we approached. I was prepared to do anything to stop him from taking it, so I swung to the right and into his horse's flank, which made him veer off course. He was furious.

"What the hell are you playing at?" he yelled in uncharacteristic rage. "We'll lose the pack!"

"Sorry Vincent – accident. I'm a bit rusty."

"Rusty? Rusty my foot! You did it on purpose!"

Jumping a low hedge farther down the field, we raced after our companions, the mud flying up from the horses' hooves, the steam rising in the cold winter air.

There was a kill that day. The fox, exhausted, tried to take refuge in a rabbit hole, but got stuck a short way in. As we galloped up, the hounds were already digging it out. Suddenly they had it, dragging it out and tearing it to pieces in seconds. Normally the sight would have sickened me, but all I felt was relief. The danger to Vincent was over. There would be no more galloping and jumping that day – just lots of congratulations and backslapping, and no one, to my knowledge, had ever died from that.

"What on earth was wrong with you out there?" Vincent asked me as we made our way home later.

"What do you mean?"

"You know exactly what I mean. You ruined my day!"

"Let's go on that long walk," I suggested, changing the subject.

He looked at me dubiously.

"Hmm. All right, we'll go on a walk. Perhaps you've got more sense in you when you're not on a horse."

I allowed myself a brief smile as he trotted away. I was almost sure that I had saved the man's life, and he was now out of harm's way.

"I know," he said eagerly, "let's take a couple of shotguns – we can shoot some snipe."

I won't relate what happened on the walk, because nothing of much interest did. Suffice to say that, just as he had survived the fox hunt, so he survived the walk, even though we took two shotguns. He survived the long tramp home. At no point did he fall over and crack his head open, as I thought he would, or suffer a heart attack, which was my constant expectation.

We sat together in the library after dinner, and I was relieved that the telephone remained silent. Jenkins came in at exactly the same time as the previous evening.

"Glass of port, sir?"

"Thank you Jenkins, yes."

By the time it got to about eleven o'clock I'd convinced myself that Alison's voice had been a trick of some sort, or a delusion, or a unique and unexplained natural phenomenon, or even a figment of my imagination. After all, half-scared out of my wits by the ringing of the disconnected telephone, what could be more natural than my brain inventing something even more scary to explain it?

As for the ringing of the phone itself, I concluded that it had to be the product of a malicious or tasteless joke. I decided to examine it when Vincent had gone to bed. If there was anything suspicious, I would ask Jenkins about it. He would have the best idea as to who the culprit was.

"Well, I'm going to bed," said Vincent eventually.

"Goodnight, Vincent."

"Goodnight. And..."

"Yes?"

"Thanks for staying on like this. I do appreciate it. I'm not used to being alone. I've barely spent a day apart from Alison in twenty years. It feels so strange."

"Yes, it's going to be difficult for a very long time, Vincent."

"Yes. I suppose it will be."

He made his way clumsily to the door – he had drunk more wine than usual at dinner – and then paused.

"That business with the phone last night..."

"Yes?"

"Don't want to sound silly, but... Well, there wasn't anyone there was there? On the other end of the line?"

"No. No, of course not."

"No, sorry. Silly to ask."

He opened the door, turned to look at me, gave me a curious half-smile, then left the room. Before examining the telephone I waited a few minutes to make sure that he wasn't coming back.

It was while I was dismantling the receiver that I heard it – a single gunshot, somewhere in the house. For some reason, the first thing I did was to look at the clock. It was one minute to midnight.

I ran out of the library and up the stairs to Vincent's bedroom. I stopped in the doorway. A man was standing over a body in the middle of the room. In his hand he was holding a gun, from which a thin wisp of smoke was still curling.

"Jenkins!"

"Yes sir," he answered, with ridiculous formality.

"Jenkins... why?"

"I'm afraid I haven't the faintest idea, sir."

"Give me the gun."

"May I place it over here instead, sir?" he said, putting it on a chest of drawers. "You might get your finger- prints on it otherwise."

Too shocked to answer, I just stared at him.

"And now sir, if you will excuse me, I think it would be appropriate if I send for the police."

He glided past without a sound and made his way downstairs. I walked into the room slowly, and looked down at Vincent lying spread-eagled on the floor, a single bullet wound in the back of his head. His eyes were closed, and there was a faint smile on his face. He looked happy and at peace. I had no doubt that he was with Alison. After all, she was expecting him.

The Shadow of a Ghost

My sister Lettie has a broken heart. There's nothing very unusual about this, of course, but no one ever suffered that fate in a stranger, more frightening way than Lettie.

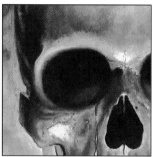

She met George Mason at a wedding, and they fell in love at first sight. He was an officer in the Navy by profession, a rather ambitious one too, so when he got the chance to go on an expedition to the Arctic, he jumped at it. The purpose of the trip was to discover the fate of Sir John Franklin, the explorer who, together with his two ships, had vanished in 1845. Lettie took a lot of persuading, because George would be away for two years, but in the end she agreed that he should go. It was a decision she has regretted ever since.

My brother Harry used to live with us in those days. He's quite a famous painter now, but then he was just a lowly student at art school. Lettie asked him to paint George's portrait before the expedition set out. Harry approached his task very seriously, making George endure half a dozen lengthy sittings, during which he expounded his main ideas on the theory of art. Maybe my brother didn't fully understand his own theories, because the finished painting was, in my opinion, terrible.

Lettie thought the portait was "exquisite and beautiful", however, while Harry pronounced it "easily my finest work to date". They bought an enormous gilt frame of the sort that usually displays renowned prime ministers or great generals. It weighed half as much as George himself, and looked quite ridiculous on our dining room wall, but as long as it made Lettie and Harry happy I didn't mind.

Three weeks before George's ship, *The Pioneer,* was due to sail, George brought a colleague to our house for dinner. His name was Vincent Grieve, and he held the title of ship's surgeon.

We greeted him in a friendly way, but I took an instant dislike to the man. He had a hard, calculating face, and there was something cruel in his expression. I didn't trust him, and the way he behaved that evening didn't do anything to change this feeling. To our amazement, he tried to flirt with Lettie, although he knew she was engaged already. Lettie made it crystal clear to him that his attention was unwelcome, while George and I dropped stronger and stronger hints that his conduct was unacceptable, but the man was incredibly thick-skinned. He seemed to have no idea how much he was offending us.

At dinner I put him between myself and my wife, Rachel. On the other side of the table, below George's portrait, were Lettie, George and Harry.

"I wonder if I might change seats with somebody?" he asked when we were halfway through the first course.

"If you wish," I said, puzzled. "You can have mine."

"I'd rather sit on that side of the table, if you don't mind," he said emphatically. "It's that portrait, you see. I don't like to look at it. It's eyes are rather... *disturbing*."

A short silence followed this peculiar comment.

"Take my seat, Mr. Grieve," Lettie offered, half standing up.

"No, no, I wouldn't dream of it," he quickly answered. "Please, I insist, I won't have you disturbed, I simply won't allow it."

"Well in that case," George muttered, "you'd better have mine."

"So kind," Grieve said, with a strange smile.

I took this as a blatant and shameless ploy to sit next to Lettie, and indeed he spent the rest of the evening trying to talk only to her.

When George was leaving that evening, I asked him if he was going to bring his colleague home with him again. He replied that although the man could be pleasant enough company on a ship, he didn't know how to behave in a home. He wouldn't be welcome any more.

But the seed had been sown. Taking advantage of the introduction to our household, Grieve didn't wait to be invited again. He called the very next day, and the day after that, and many days following, and soon he was a more frequent visitor than George himself.

I would have told Grieve not to visit, but he was a very slippery customer, and he always seemed to have some legitimate excuse. He often brought, or pretended to bring, some little message from George. Anyway, as *The Pioneer* would be leaving soon, it seemed best just to put up with the situation.

The day before the ship sailed, Grieve did something unforgivable. He managed to get Lettie on her own, and he told her that he loved her. He said he knew that she was already engaged, but that didn't stop another man from loving her too. Lettie was furious and ordered him out of the house. Yet even on the doorstep, as she tried to shut the door on him, he persisted, grabbing her hand against her will.

"Two years is a long time," he whispered to her, "and who knows whether George will still love you at the end of it!"

"You— How *dare* you!"

"Then you will remember, my darling, that I love you a million times more than he does!"

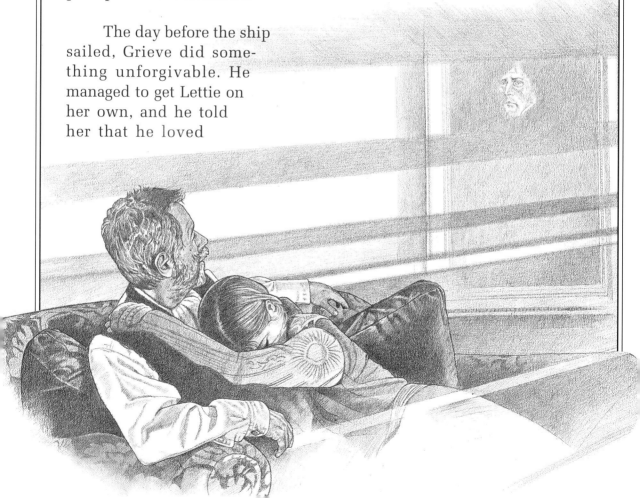

I was very angry when she told me about this incident, but Lettie persuaded me not to confront Grieve about it. The ship was sailing the next day, so she didn't think it was worth causing any trouble.

Lettie cried her eyes out that evening, and George wasn't much better. They were deeply in love, and the thought of not seeing each other for two years, maybe more, was almost unbearable.

"Don't go!" I heard Lettie weep as I was passing the sitting room. "Please, please don't go!"

"I love you, but I must go!" George said, his voice breaking, as Lettie's crying became even louder.

I moved on, shaking my head sadly. The thought of Lettie being so unhappy made me unhappy too, and I wished that George wasn't so ambitious and adventurous. Why couldn't he just stay at home and work in an office, like me?

The two lovers talked until dawn,when George had to tear himself away. I was there to comfort Lettie. I led her away from the open front door, where she had been standing, shivering, for ten minutes, and into the dining room. I sat her down on a sofa. All I could do was be there for her as she sobbed on my shoulder, or stared adoringly at the portrait of the man she loved.

Lettie received two letters from George over the next few months. In the second he said that he wouldn't be able to write again. *The Pioneer* was about to enter very high latitudes, where only exploratory missions went, and it was unlikely they would encounter any ships that could bring letters back. There was a long silence, and an anxious, lonely year for Lettie.

We heard of the expedition once in the papers. A returning Russian expedition had come across them. Their ship was stranded in ice for the winter, but they planned to continue the search for Franklin on foot across the frozen wastes.

Winter passed, and spring came. One evening, an unusually warm one, we were all sitting in the dining room after an early dinner – Lettie, Harry, Rachel, and myself. Harry was looking out of the window aimlessly. Rachel and I were writing letters. Lettie was sitting silently on the sofa. It was an ordinary evening.

Suddenly a chill seemed to sweep into the room. It wasn't the wind or a breeze, because the curtains didn't move. It was like a feeling of deathly cold, which stayed for just a few seconds. I looked up, almost in alarm, as its icy fingers brushed across me. Lettie was shivering.

"Perhaps we're having a taste of George's polar weather," I joked.

My wife stared at me in a faintly puzzled way, as did Harry.

I glanced up at George's portrait... the shock was so intense that I couldn't even gasp. A sort of feverish, panicked heat replaced the previous feeling of icy cold, because I saw, in the place of George's head, a weeping skull. I stared at it hard, almost willing it to go away, but there was no denying the empty eye sockets, the gleaming teeth, the fleshless cheekbones. It was the face of death.

Without saying a word, I got up from my chair and walked straight over to the painting. As I drew nearer, a mist seemed to pass across it, and when I was standing close, all I could see was George's face. The horrible spectral skull had faded away and vanished.

"Poor George," I whispered unconsciously.

Lettie looked up. If the tone of my voice hadn't alarmed her, the look on my face did. Her eyes grew wide in fear.

"What do you mean?" she said breathlessly. "Have you heard anything?"

"No, no, of course not Lettie, nothing at all, I just—"

"Oh Robert, tell me what you've heard!"

"Nothing at all, I promise you. I was just thinking about him, that's all, and about the hardship he must be experiencing. It must have been that sudden cold feeling that did it."

"Cold feeling!" exclaimed my brother by the window. "Cold feeling! How on earth could you feel cold on a sweltering evening like this?"

"There was a sudden chill in the air earlier," I said, becoming slightly irritated. "I'm surprised you didn't feel it yourself. It passed through the room."

"Robert, are you feeling all right?" my wife asked. "It's very warm tonight, very warm indeed. Perhaps you're coming down with flu. Do you have a temperature."

"You didn't feel cold?"

"No, my dear."

Lettie, pale and wide-eyed, was staring at me.

"I did," she said quietly, and left the room. Rachel, much confused, hurried after her.

"What's the date, Harry?" I asked, after a moment's thought.

"The twenty-third of May. Why do you want to know?"

I told him to make a note of it in his diary, but I refused to say any more than that.

"You and Lettie are both as mad as each other," he said.

I saw, in the place of George's head, a weeping skull

Lettie and I never mentioned what occurred that night. But deep down I was convinced that something terrible had happened to George, and from that day on, though I hoped against hope that I was wrong, I dreaded the arrival of bad news. At last the day came, as I knew it would.

I was lingering over my breakfast that morning when Harry came bursting into the dining room. He looked flushed and agitated.

"Is she down yet?" he asked.

"Who?"

"Lettie."

"No."

"Robert, something awful has happened!" he cried, handing me a page torn from *The Daily News*.

PIONEER FAILS TO FIND FRANKLIN

OFFICER'S DEATH ENDS DOOMED POLAR TRIP

The expedition to discover the fate of Captain Franklin has failed. *The Pioneer,* a British ship which set out eighteen months ago, has been forced to turn back. The crew is suffering from hunger, exhaustion and lack of supplies. One member of the crew is reported to have died. He was George Mason, a young officer.

The Pioneer is the third expedition that has tried to trace Captain Franklin, who disappeared in...

Harry and I looked at each other with tears in our eyes.

"Poor George."

"Poor Lettie."

"We mustn't let her see this," my brother said.

"Oh, how are we going to tell her?" I cried.

At that moment Harry clutched at my arm.

"Hush!"

I turned to the door. There was Lettie, her face as pale as death and an expression of absolute despair in her eyes. I don't know how much

she had heard, but it was enough. I sprang forward, but she waved me away, turned around, and went straight back upstairs.

Since that day, I have never heard her laugh, or seen her smile.

Months passed. I read in the paper that *The Pioneer* had arrived back in England, but I didn't tell anyone. The expedition was of no interest to any of us now, and just the mention of its name would cause Lettie a great deal of pain.

One afternoon shortly after this there was a loud knock at the front door. When our servant opened it, I heard a voice I recognized but couldn't quite place. The servant came into the room and handed me a visiting card which said: *Vincent Grieve, Surgeon.*

"Show him in," I said. "And if your mistress and Miss Lettie return, tell them I have someone with me on business and don't want to be disturbed."

I was relieved that Lettie was out. I went into the hall to meet Grieve, who was changed, horribly changed. He was paler than ever, hollow-eyed and hollow-cheeked, and had acquired a strange stoop. His eyes, which once looked so crafty and cunning, now looked merely frightened, like those of a hunted beast. Three times in the space of a few seconds he looked over his shoulder, as if afraid that something was following him. In truth, I felt an absolute repugnance for him. I visibly shuddered as we shook hands.

"The expedition was one of terrible hardship," I said, trying to sound sympathetic.

"I wish I'd never gone on it," he answered in a fierce, half-mad whisper.

"Well, come into the dining room."

He grabbed my arm.

"Is the portrait still there?"

"Of course."

"Cover it up!" he begged.

"What?"

"Cover it up!"

"All right," I replied, after a moment's hesitation.

Wondering what on earth had made me agree to this odd request, I went into the dining room first and put a tablecloth over the picture.

I was very blunt. I said that I was glad to see him safely returned, and would be grateful to hear how George had died. However, I told him that he couldn't see Lettie, and should never call at our house again. He took this quietly, sinking slowly down onto the sofa and sighing deeply. He looked so very weak and drained that I offered him a glass of wine, which he greedily drank down. He stayed silent until I asked him about George's death.

The story was told nervously, in a low, halting voice. I noticed that he continually looked to one side, almost as if he were scared of someone overhearing him. He described how, on the long trek back across the ice to the ship, when the crew was close to starvation, they had spotted a polar bear about a mile away, on shifting ice. A polar bear would have been the difference between life and death to the crew of *The Pioneer*. He and George volunteered to hunt it.

The conditions were very dangerous, and they had to take extreme

care on the treacherous icebergs, leaving their heavy fur coats behind to give themselves extra agility. One particular iceberg was ridged like the roof of a house, with a smooth, treacherous slope on one side that descended to the edge of a great precipice. They scrambled up to the top of the ridge and started to crawl along it. But George momentarily lost his concentration, and his footing.

"I shouted," Grieve said in a hoarse whisper, "but it was too late. The surface was like glass. George tried to fling himself back onto the ridge, but he slipped onto his knees and went farther down the slope. I stretched out my hands – he couldn't reach. He was slipping down the icy slope. There was something... horrible in that long, slow slide. Horrible. I watched him. He pulled his gloves off and

tried to dig his fingernails in to the ice, but it had no effect. I shouted again, but there was nothing I could do. He was sliding ever closer to the edge of the precipice."

Grieve paused, wiping his sweating brow with a handkerchief. He hesitated before continuing, and I thought I saw the old cunning look in his eyes again.

"George knew he was moments away from death," Grieve said in a quiet whisper. "He called out to me. With the last words he ever spoke he told me to come here when I got back, and say goodbye! To you, and, and to her!"

His voice broke. He struggled to regain control over himself.

"He told me to promise. I did as he asked, and he disappeared over the edge forever. A prayer came to my lips, and—"

Grieve's jaw had suddenly dropped in amazement, and his eyeballs almost sprang out of his head.

He pointed at the portrait behind me and screamed like an animal caught in a snare, before dropping on the floor to his knees.

"Cover it up!" he shrieked.

I turned to the portrait. The tablecloth had somehow slipped, and George's face stared out of the background with a new, accusing expression. Down his cheeks were flowing tears – tears of blood!

"Get out!" I shouted at the cowering creature that was Vincent Grieve. "Get out!"

"Your, your sister is not here?" he asked in a tortured whisper.

"No. Now go. Go, and never come back."

I virtually picked him up and dragged him to the front door.

"Wait," I called, just before pushing him out of my house, "tell me one thing. When exactly did George die?"

"Why?"

"Just tell me."

"The twenty-third of May."

He staggered down the garden path just as Harry arrived back home from art school. I didn't explain what had happened. Who would believe what I had seen in George's portrait? I shuddered when I remembered the twenty-third of May, when that icy feeling had swept through Lettie and me; at that very moment, thousands of miles away in the lonely, frozen wastes of the Arctic, George had fallen to his death.

Harry and I watched as the loathsome man crept furtively away

"My God," I suddenly breathed.

"What is it?"

"Can you see anything strange

about him at the moment?" I asked my brother.

"No, just his nasty, cowed way of walking, and the— Robert! He has a double shadow!"

It was true. Two shadows were following his departing figure. That was why he glanced behind him continually. He was being followed by something, something which no one could see, but which cast its own shadow.

Two day's later, I returned home from a walk and found the household in total confusion. Vincent Grieve had visited us again. Unfortunately, my wife had been upstairs at the time, and

Harry was at his studio. Without waiting for the servant to announce him, Grieve had walked straight into the dining room, where Lettie was reading. Apparently he had edged anxiously along the wall with the portrait on it, then sat directly under the painting so that he didn't have to look at it.

Grieve was unwell and in a state of absolute exhaustion, but he insisted on declaring to Lettie that he loved her. She angrily rejected him. But he told her that it was George's dying wish that he, Vincent Grieve, should comfort her in her grief, help her to recover, and then, eventually, marry her.

Lettie stared at his thin face and his mad, desperate eyes, utterly appalled. At that moment came a *snap!* from above. He looked up, to see George's portrait plummeting down the wall. It struck him on the head heavily and knocked him to the floor. When Rachel entered the room a few seconds later, to find Grieve unconscious, Lettie was still staring at the man in horror. Rachel sent for a doctor, and now Grieve was being tended in a spare room on the third floor.

I was livid. I ran upstairs with the intention of ordering him to get out of my house, but the man was delirious. The doctor explained that Grieve was in a critical condition, and that to move him might be fatal. In other words, I had to provide a bed for this miserable specimen of humanity, perhaps for days or even weeks. It was a repulsive idea, and I immediately employed a nurse, so that my family could avoid him completely.

Grieve left our house even sooner than I hoped. In the middle of that night a scream pierced the darkness and my sleep. I rushed to Grieve's room, where the sound had come from. Standing outside it, hugging each other in terror, were Lettie and the nurse.

Opening the door and glancing inside, I saw him sitting up in bed, completely crazed. I shut the door and locked it, then tried to calm Lettie and the nurse down. My wife and Harry arrived. We led the two distraught women downstairs and made them tea. Eventually Lettie was calm enough to tell us what had happened.

The nurse had come into her room, complaining that she was too scared to watch over her patient because he had two shadows. Lettie had agreed to go and see for herself. When they went into his room, she could see that the nurse was right;

the flickering candlelight appeared to cast two shadows of Vincent Grieve on the wall. It was as she was looking down at him in a mixture of wonder and horror that he opened his eyes. There was such a burden of suffering and guilt in his look that she felt forced to return his gaze.

"It was the memory of your face that made me do it!" he hissed. "We were at the top of the ridge. I pushed him. He fell onto the wrong side of the ridge. Then I realized what I had done, so I held out my hands to, to help him! To save him! He was slipping away, but I just grasped his fingertips. We stayed like that, catching our breath. Then we looked at each other, and I..."

"You what?" Lettie whispered.

"There, in front of my eyes, was the face of the man *you* loved," Grieve groaned, "and I hated him! If it wasn't for him, you'd love me!"

"No!"

"I let go of one of his hands. His body shifted on the ice. I waited for a moment. If he had shouted, or screamed, or begged... But he was so calm. I let go of his other hand. He slid away from me. He slid away, slowly, slowly, and all the time he was staring at me, staring at me, all the time, until—"

"Until what?"

"Until he slipped over the edge of the precipice!"

Grieve had suddenly pointed at something Lettie couldn't see, the thing that was casting the second shadow on the wall.

"But that didn't stop him – he's still staring at me! He never stops! He never leaves me! He'll be staring at me until I die!"

It was at this point that Lettie had run screaming from the room.

I was no longer prepared to have this *murderer* in my house, not under any circumstances. I ran up the stairs. I'm not sure what I meant to do – take him to the police station, or just throw him out of the front door, I neither knew nor cared. As I was fumbling to unlock his room, I could hear him screaming inside.

"No, don't – I beg you! Don't let go! No! No-ooooooo!"

I burst into the room to find the bed empty and the window wide open. I rushed over to it. He was sliding slowly, inexorably, down the wet, black slope of the roof. His fingers were scrabbling frantically at the tiles, his nails scratching against them horribly. He was looking up, apparently at me, but I couldn't help feeling that he was looking straight through me at someone else.

"Stop staring at me!" he screamed.

He slipped over the edge of the roof, and fell to his death below.

"If he had shouted, or screamed, or begged..."

A Fatal Promise

Half the young men in the village were in love with May Forster. She was the nicest girl by far – intelligent, pretty and funny, not to mention rich. She was as polite to farm workers out in the fields as to the sons of a lord at a ball. I would have proposed to her myself if I thought she might say yes, but I was convinced she'd end up with some stunningly handsome, obscenely wealthy aristocrat. I never even attempted to court her, though lots of my friends did, especially John Charrington.

Just the thought of John Charrington marrying May Forster used to make me laugh. He was a pleasant enough sort of man, but he wasn't much to look at, and he could be a bit slow at times. He wasn't exactly a barrel of laughs, either. And yet I'll say this about him: whenever he set out to do something, he generally did it. He was like a little terrier, never giving up, holding on grimly no matter what anyone told him.

He first asked her to marry him when he was twenty one. She refused. He asked her again two years later. She refused again. When he asked her for a third time, just after he'd bought a small farm, not only did she refuse, she told him never to ask her again. She went even further – she said that she didn't want to hurt his feelings, but she'd rather live on a desert island all by herself than contemplate a life married to him.

Poor old John. We all felt a bit sorry for him, although it was his own fault. If someone doesn't love you, they don't love you, so there's no point making yourself into a laughing stock.

A few months after this he came into the local inn, where some of us used to meet on a Saturday evening, looking more than unusually pleased with himself.

"Are you doing anything on Saturday the fourth of September?" he asked me.

"Haven't a clue," I answered. "It's months away."

"The thing is, I want to ask you something."

"What is it?"

He smiled at me, a great big beam that looked a bit strange on that face of his, which was usually so grave.

"Well?" I asked.

"Will you be my best man?"

After I got over the initial shock I shook him firmly by the hand and announced the good news.

"John's getting married!"

Everyone clustered around, clapping him on the back, and someone went to the bar to see if there was any champagne. I was really delighted, because for some time I'd been thinking about what a fool he was making himself look over May Forster. "There are plenty of other fish in the sea," I used to tell him, to which he always replied, rather pompously: "No, Peter, there's only one fish in the sea." Now it looked as though he'd come around to my way of thinking.

The champagne appeared. I opened it myself after giving the bottle a good shake, so that for a minute everyone was holding out their glasses and laughing.

"Who's the lucky girl, John?" someone called.

"May Forster," he said.

There was a brief silence before we all burst out laughing. It wasn't like John to tell a joke, but when he did it was always a good one.

"But it's true!" he said.

"You don't mean it?" I asked.

"Of course I mean it," he told me, frowning, as though he was completely astonished that I could doubt it. "Didn't I always say I'd marry May Forster?"

"Yes, but—"

"Well now you know the day: Saturday the fourth of September."

We all began clapping him on the back once more, as if the fact of marrying May Forster, as opposed to anyone else, required a new and even more enthusiastic display of congratulations.

"What does she see in you, John?" joked James Giles, although perhaps there was an edge to the question – he'd once been turned down by May himself.

"Don't you know?"

"No," said James, to general laughter.

In all honesty, I could see his point of view. He was all the things that John wasn't: clever, witty and good-looking. It was ridiculous to think that May would prefer to marry John, who was rather plain and ordinary and, well, boring.

"Well I'll tell you," John said calmly, and in such a way that we all leaned forward and listened more carefully, as though we might learn something: "I never, *ever*, give up."

I thought a lot about John and May in the next week. I couldn't help feeling that she was making a big mistake. To marry a man merely because he wouldn't stop pestering you didn't seem much of a reason. Where was the love? Where was the passion? How were they going to live together for the rest of their lives? But the next time I saw May I stopped asking questions like that.

She blushed like a schoolgirl when I congratulated her, and tears of happiness – yes, *tears* – formed in her eyes, as though she could scarcely believe her luck in marrying such a wonderful man. I was left in no doubt that she adored him.

Something else happened at that time which revealed John in a new light to me. I was walking home one summer evening, after a very enjoyable time at the inn with my friends, and I decided to take a short cut through the churchyard. I climbed over the wall and began threading my way through the graves to the other side.

I saw May, sitting on a flat tomb, with the full glory of the evening light illuminating her face, filtering through her rich, chestnut-brown hair. She was so breathtakingly beautiful that I just stopped in my tracks and stared. John was lying down in the grass at her feet. Her expression was so tender and loving that a kind of regret swept through me, a regret that she didn't love *me.*

"Darling!" I heard John say. "Nothing could take me away from you! I'd come back from the dead for you if I had to!"

I didn't know he was capable of such passion, and I stole away from the scene quietly, very moved. My opinion of their relationship was utterly revised. They were head over heels in love.

July and August passed, and the wedding drew near. Two days before the actual day I had to go to Oxford on business. The train was late. I was standing on the platform, looking at my pocket watch and grumbling to myself, when I saw John and May. They were walking up and down at the far end of the platform, arm in arm and oblivious to the bustle all around them. I didn't want to interrupt, so I buried my nose in a newspaper until the

"I'd come back from the dead for you if I had to!"

train arrived. John got on but May stayed behind.

"Hello!" John exclaimed when he saw me – I'd walked up through the train until I found him.

"Where are you off to?" I asked.

"Visiting Mr. Banbridge, my godfather," he replied, before leaning out of the window to talk to May.

I saw that her eyes were red-rimmed, and I was struck once again, and not without a tinge of envy, by the intensity of her love.

"I wish you wouldn't go, John," I heard her say, "not just before the wedding like this. What if something happens?"

"Do you think I'd let anything stop our wedding?" he asked. "No chance! Try not to worry, May."

"Don't go," she whispered just as the train started to pull away, and in such a pleading way that, if she had been talking to me, I would have thrown my suitcase out of the window and jumped after it.

But John had decided to go, and once he had decided to do something he never changed his mind.

"I'll be back tomorrow," he called, "or definitely on Saturday in time for the wedding! I promise!"

The train built up speed, and soon May was just a small figure in a cloud of steam, waving.

"I'm afraid Mr. Banbridge is really ill," John said glumly, sitting back, "and he's sent for me, so I feel I have to go. He's been very good to me over the years, and as I said to May, I'll be back in time."

"But what if... what if Mr. Banbridge dies, John?"

"Alive or dead, I mean to be married on Saturday!"

He opened the newspaper, rather grumpily, and started to do the crossword. Two hours later, when the train pulled into Oxford, he'd only completed a few clues, but he was still working at it doggedly.

"It might take weeks, but I'll finish this crossword!" he claimed.

That was the sort of man he was, ridiculous and impressive, both at the same time.

When I got back from Oxford late the following day the first thing I did was go to John's house. I wanted to reassure myself that he was back. It's the sort of thing you like to know when you're going to be a best man the following afternoon. Well, he wasn't there, but at home there was a letter waiting for me.

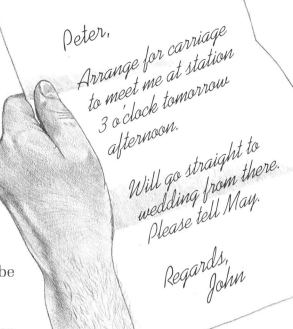

Peter,

Arrange for carriage to meet me at station 3 o'clock tomorrow afternoon.

Will go straight to wedding from there. Please tell May.

Regards,
John

Three o'clock! He intended to arrive with only half an hour to spare! In one sense it was a relief to know his plans, but that letter also made me very angry. Half an hour left no margin for error, and it seemed like an insult to May to take a risk like that.

If May was upset or annoyed, she didn't show it. I explained that John and I would come straight to the church from the station.

"He's so good," she said. "He wouldn't have the heart to turn Mr. Banbridge down. Only... he *will* turn up on time, Peter, won't he?"

I reassured May that there was no doubt about this, although I was far from certain myself, and after trying to cheer her up with some chatter and a couple of jokes about married life, I said goodnight and went home to bed.

The fourth of September was the longest day of my life. I woke up early, with butterflies in my stomach, and spent the morning pacing up and down restlessly. I'd start to read a book, and then realize I'd been looking at the same page for five minutes without taking in a word of it; or I'd take a stroll in the garden to check how the vegetables were doing, then completely forget why I'd gone out there.

Old Tom Stringham was in the garden, a man who did some work for me occasionally. I'm afraid I was a bit sharp with him, telling him off for something that wasn't his fault.

"Very well, sir," he answered, so meekly that it made me feel guilty.

"Sorry Tom – didn't mean to snap. I'm just a little nervous about this wedding."

"I'm sure you'll be fine, sir. Happy with your speech?"

"Yes, yes, I'm not worried about that. It's John I'm worried about. What if he doesn't make it?"

"Don't you bother yourself with Mr. Charrington, sir. Why, you can set your watch by that man."

"That's true."

"Mark my words sir, John Charrington won't be late."

"Yes. Thank you Tom."

"Happy to oblige, sir, and good luck to you. I may walk up to the church myself later on."

"Perhaps I'll see you there."

At the station at half-past two, in my top hat and tails, I attracted several admiring glances. The sky, which had been a brilliant blue all morning, was taking on a threatening aspect, but I was far too preoccupied with John's imminent arrival to worry about rain. My eyes were fixed on the hands of the old clock that hung down over the platform. Never, in my entire life, have I seen a clock measure out time more slowly. By the time it chimed three, I was extremely tense.

The train was late. I stood on the edge of the platform, looking along the track for the first sight of it. It seemed like ages before I saw a puff of steam in the distance. As I strained to see, the engine gradually came into view, although at such a sluggish pace that I was cursing the driver in my mind. It seemed to creep into the station, as though the driver could barely be bothered to make the last few yards. But at last it had arrived, and I could, at last, stop worrying about John, and start worrying about ordinary things, such as if I had the ring, and whether my speech would go down well at the reception.

The doors swung open to let out all the passengers, who piled up their luggage in heaps and hailed porters. The doors banged shut. I couldn't see John, but the platform was crowded, and I thought he'd appear at my side at any moment. But as the people dispersed, no John appeared. I *willed* him to be there, to emerge from a carriage or a cluster of people and put my fears to rest, but fewer and fewer people were left on the platform. The train steamed out of the station. He had missed it.

I was livid. What a fool he was! It was ten past three, and there wasn't another train for over half an hour. Even if we drove like the wind, we would be at least forty-five minutes late. I was very angry, more for May than for me. He had no right to treat her so badly.

If things seemed grim then, they looked even worse when the next train arrived. John wasn't on that one either. I rushed out of the station and leaped into the carriage. "Drive to the church!"

Anxiety replaced anger. What on earth had become of him? Had he been taken ill? In which case, why didn't he send a telegram? Had there been an accident? I grimaced when I thought of the news I was going to have to break to May and her family, waiting at the church with all their friends.

It was five past four when, the sky now heavy with ominous black clouds, the carriage drew up at the churchyard gate. I was surprised to see a crowd of eager onlookers outside the door; it was as though they were waiting for the happy couple to emerge from the church, which was, of course, impossible. I hurried up to them in a mad panic, hearing comments such as 'That's the best man' and 'Better late than never!' as I approached. Just to the left I saw my gardener, Tom, and – perhaps because I wasn't looking forward to facing May and telling her that there wasn't going to be a wedding – I paused to speak to him.

"A sorry mess, Tom, isn't it?" I whispered.

"Yes indeed, sir. Sorry you're late, sir. Sure it wasn't your fault."

"*Me* late? It's John, not me. He wasn't at the station."

"But he's here, sir."

"*Here?*"

"Yes sir, arrived at half-past three on the dot. You can set your watch by John Charrington."

A feeling of intense dismay flooded through me as I thought that whatever had happened must have somehow been my fault, and that I had ruined the wedding.

"It's probably all over by now," Tom continued. "They asked James Giles to step into your shoes."

While I was still reeling, Tom touched me on the elbow and began to whisper in my ear discreetly.

"Between you and me, something's gone badly wrong. Not just you being late sir, if you'll excuse me for saying so, but Mr. Charrington

looked mighty peculiar."

"What are you saying, Tom?"

"I think he's been drinking."

"*Drinking?*"

"Yes sir. I think he's been drinking a lot. He turned up here all dirty and dusty, as if he'd taken a tumble, sir, and his face was as white as a sheet, with a nasty mark on the forehead. He walked up this here path, sir, as you are standing on now, in a mighty strange manner, and in he went with his eyes fixed straight ahead, white as a ghost – not a glance or a word for any of us, and him being such a down-to-earth and friendly sort of man as a rule, sir."

I'd never heard Tom make such a long speech. I was just preparing to slip into the church and salvage what I could from the situation, when I noticed the crowd shifting and straining to see what was going on, and I realized that the newly-married couple were about to come out. All down the path the waiting villagers were holding handfuls of rice to throw over John and May, and from the bell tower above came the lilting peal of the wedding bells.

Out they came. Looking just as Tom had described him, if not even worse, John walked slowly past. I tried to catch his eye, but he glanced neither left nor right. He looked so ghastly that the crowd hesitated, not

I hurried up to them in a mad panic

sure whether to throw their rice, and a mood of intense gloom seemed to settle over everyone, pervading the churchyard with a feeling almost of despair. It was at that instant that the cheery wedding peal petered out, replaced, within a few seconds, by a sound which made my heart stop: a single, mournful,

The bell ringers suddenly came tumbling out of the church door, panic etched on their faces, pushing the relatives of the bride and groom out of their way.

"You should be ashamed of yourselves!" someone in the crowd shouted at them.

tolling bell; the grim knell of a funeral... I looked at May, holding onto John's arm and staring down blankly at the ground. She was shivering, as though utterly freezing, and she was almost as ashen as he was. Her wedding dress of white silk added to the effect, so that the only part of her which wasn't deathly-pale was her dark-brown hair. She looked like she was in a state of shock.

"It's not us!" one of them replied. "We don't know what happened, we were just, we— the bells are playing themselves! There's no one up there!"

Apparently oblivious to the confusion and fear that this claim provoked, John and May reached the end of the path and climbed into the carriage waiting to take them to the reception. The door slammed shut behind them.

"May God have mercy on them," I heard old Tom whisper in a hoarse voice.

Half the crowd began to babble and talk, while the other half walked away in frightened silence, some crossing themselves. I suddenly found Mr. Forster, May's father, standing at my side.

"If I'd seen him in that state before the service I'd have called the whole thing off," he muttered. "And you, Peter – how did you allow him to arrive in that condition? Why were you late?"

"I'm so sorry, I—"

"Never mind. The damage has been done."

He marched away and went to comfort his wife, who was crying quietly by the church door.

I was feeling quite ill from a mixture of emotions: shame and embarrassment at missing the service, and, well, outright *fear* about John and May. What on earth was going on? Even so, I decided that I had to do the best I could from that point on, and I began to escort people into the carriages that were to take them to the reception. In a few minutes the carriages were full, and we were ready to set off.

The bride and groom's carriage went first, with the other carriages following. However, the pace was so slow that it was like being in a funeral cortège rather than a wedding procession. I was with May's family in the second carriage, and I shouted to the driver of the first to speed up.

"I'm doing my best sir," he called back in a puzzled voice, "but it's the horses – they won't go any faster!"

We took the decision to overtake the carriage, and I gestured to the carriages behind ours to follow. We thought that if the guests were already waiting at the reception to welcome the bride and groom, it would create a better atmosphere, and the rest of the day might pass off more successfully than the actual wedding had.

As we passed the front carriage I couldn't help looking in, but there was nothing to see. The curtain was drawn. The pace of the horses was painfully slow. The driver shook the reins, becoming quite angry, yet the horses took no notice of him whatsoever, as though they were being led by an outside force. This only added to the sense of uneasiness and confusion we all felt.

At May's house all the guests assembled on the steps outside the front door, and in the gravel driveway, some of us doing our best to seem chatty and cheerful. But above us, rolling storm clouds rumbled, and nothing could dispel the deep feeling of gloom I felt inside. This feeling only intensified when the bride and groom's carriage finally came crunching up the drive to stop in front of us. Mr. Forster and I walked forward. The curtain, which had been closed before, was now drawn back, revealing... revealing nothing.

"Coachman, it's empty!" Mr. Forster exclaimed.

"But I drove straight here, sir," the coachman answered, "and I swear there wasn't anyone got out."

Mr. Forster opened the door. For some moments we just stared at the scene inside. The carriage wasn't empty. May was cowering on the floor, her hands clamped over her face, staring out of the gaps between her fingers with wild, unseeing eyes. John was nowhere to be seen.

"May!" shouted her father in a strangled cry, lifting her out of the carriage.

I looked at her, half-dead in his arms. She was white, so white, her face engraved with horror, the face of someone who has stared into the eyes of the unknown. I have never before witnessed such desolation. I hope I never will again. As for her hair, her shining, dark-brown,

lovely hair... every strand of it was as white as snow.

A tremendous crack of thunder overhead broke the stillness, and signified the start of utter chaos. May's mother fainted, collapsing to the ground, and suddenly, as rain fell out of the sky to drench us in seconds, everyone was shouting or screaming or running around madly. Some went off to call for a doctor, and still more were just screaming out of pure, hysterical terror. In the middle of it, Mr. Forster and I stood silent and unmoving, he with his daughter lying limply in his arms, tears streaming down his cheeks.

I felt someone tugging at my elbow. Looking down, I saw a small boy, frightened and bewildered, holding up a piece of paper.

"Are you Mr. Templer, sir?"

"What? Yes."

"Telegram, sir."

"What?"

"Telegram."

I took it from him mechanically, my senses so battered by tragedy and baffled by the inexplicable that I was barely aware of what I was doing. The boy stared up at me, waiting.

"Aren't you going to read it sir?"

"What? Oh, yes, yes of course."

I opened it. My eyes ranged across the words without taking in their meaning, the letters seemed to swim around in front of me. I shook my head, narrowed my eyes and, with great difficulty, started to read.

HEARTBREAKING NEWS...JOHN THROWN FROM HORSE ON WAY TO OXFORD STATION AT ONE O'CLOCK...DIED INSTANTLY...SENDING THIS IN HOPE THAT YOU RECEIVE IT BEFORE WEDDING...PROFOUND SYMPATHIES TO MAY AND FAMILY...MRS BANBRIDGE...

He died in Oxford at one o'clock – and he was married to May Forster at half-past three, in the presence of half the village! What happened in the carriage on the way to May's house? No one knows. No one ever will. They brought John Charrington's body from Oxford and buried him in the churchyard. As for May, she never regained consciousness again. She died of shock, and was buried next to him.

The graves were near the spot where I'd seen May and John only a few months before, when May looked more beautiful than it's possible to imagine, and John made what turned out to be a fatal promise: that if he had to, he would come back from the dead for her.

The Four-Fifteen Express

In 1857, after a six month trip to Poland and the Baltic States, I returned to England to spend Christmas with my good friends Isobel and Jonathan Jelf at Dumbleton, which is near Clayborough. I usually spent Christmas with my friends and I have many happy memories of those times, and yet, as it turned out, my memories of Christmas in 1857 weren't to be quite so pleasant.

Clayborough lies on the East Anglian Line which runs from London to Crampton. I arrived at the station in London with plenty of time to spare. It was the fourth of December, a cold and foggy day.

Wanting a compartment to myself, I had a quiet word with the guard, a big, ruddy-faced fellow with a fine set of whiskers. He led me down the platform to an empty compartment and gave me a key, telling me to lock the door so no one else could get in. When I got out at Clayborough, I was to leave the key under the seat. I was more than happy with this arrangement, because I was rather tired and didn't feel like making polite small talk with strangers.

I have to admit to a feeling of smugness when, glancing outside, I saw a hunched figure hurrying along the carriage. At least he couldn't get into *my* compartment. As if to confirm this, he stopped outside the door and rattled the handle. To my great astonishment, however, *he* had a key as well.

As soon as I got a clear look at him I realized I knew him. He was a tall man, thin-lipped and stooping, with a gloomy expression. He had a large, battered document case, which he carefully placed under his seat. Several times I saw him pat the outside of his jacket, as though checking that something in an inside pocket was still there.

He was John Derry, a lawyer I had met at Dumbleton three years before. Isobel was his cousin. I couldn't help thinking that time had been unkind to him since we last saw each other. He was very pale, almost alarmingly pale, with a restless, anguished look in his eyes, but when we started to talk he gave no hint that anything was wrong.

"Mr. Derry, isn't it?"

"Yes, that's right."

"I had the pleasure of meeting you at Dumbleton a few years ago."

"I thought I recognized you," he said, peering at me closely. "I'm afraid I've forgotten your..."

"Langford, William Langford. I've known Jonathan and Isobel for years. I'm spending Christmas with them. Perhaps you are too?"

"Oh no, not me," said Mr. Derry, puffing out his chest with an air of self-importance. "I'm engaged on crucial business concerning the new branch line from Blackwater to Stockbridge, which you'll know about, of course."

I explained that I had been out of the country for some time and had no knowledge of it.

"I'm very surprised," he said in a reproving voice, as if everyone in Poland and the Baltic States must have been talking about little else. "Stockbridge needs a branch line if it's to remain a flourishing town, and I've been overseeing the project. I'm one of the directors of the East Anglian Line," he said proudly.

Talkative, pompous, obsessed with the new branch line from Blackwater to Stockbridge, Mr. Derry methodically outlined the main obstacles he had met during the course of his work: the greed of the land- owners,

I was struggling against a tidal wave of sleep and boredom

the indifference of the people of Stockbridge, the objections of the local newspaper, each of which Mr. Derry elaborated on in merciless, mind-numbing detail.

In less than ten minutes I was struggling against a tidal wave of sleep and boredom. My companion, oblivious to the enormous yawns that were overpowering me, went on to tell me even more information about the proposed new branch line, until my head ached and my eyelids quivered with fatigue. At length I was roused by these words:

"Seventy-five thousand pounds, *cash down.*"

"Seventy-five thousand," I said, in as lively a voice as I could manage, "*cash down.*"

"A large sum to carry around," he said in a whisper, patting the left side of his jacket.

That revived me a bit.

"You don't mean to say you have seventy-five thousand pounds in your pocket?" I exclaimed.

"My good sir," said Mr. Derry in great irritation, "didn't I first tell you that fact not forty-five minutes ago? The seventy-five thousand pounds has to be handed over to a Stockbridge landowner by half-past seven this evening."

"But how will you get to Stockbridge from Blackwater by half-past seven? There *isn't* a branch line between those towns yet."

"To Stockbridge?" echoed the lawyer, as if I had just expressed the most extraordinary opinion he had ever heard in his entire life. "To Stockbridge? I thought I'd explained to you that the landowner's lawyer has offices in Mallingford, which is less than a mile from Blackwater. Obviously I will walk."

"I'm sorry," I stammered, "I must have misunderstood."

"I think you must."

"Would you like me to take a message to your cousin?" I asked, in an attempt to get him off the subject of his cherished railway.

"You may wish her," he said, "a very merry Christmas. And you may advise her," he added after a moment's thought, chuckling to himself, "not to burn down the blue bedroom while someone is staying in it. It is *not* a very festive act."

"There was a fire in your room once?"

"There was indeed, and very unpleasant it was. Are we here?" he observed as the train slowed down. "Time has *flown* past."

Not for me it hadn't. I was glad to see the back of him. As he put on his coat, the door which connected the compartment with the corridor opened and the guard with the ruddy face and big whiskers came in.

"Tickets please!"

"I'm going to Clayborough," I said.

"Very well, sir," he answered, checking my ticket before going out into the corridor again.

"He didn't ask to see yours," I said to Mr. Derry in surprise.

"They never do," he replied. "I travel free. Everyone on the East Anglian Line knows who I am."

"Blackwater! Blackwater!" shouted a porter on the platform as the train drew into the station.

"It's been *extremely* interesting talking to you," said Mr. Derry, which was no doubt true – for him. "Good evening."

"Good evening," I replied, holding out my hand.

He hesitated so emphatically that I found myself looking down at my hand, as if there were something wrong with it. For some reason, Derry wouldn't, or couldn't, shake it. Instead he lifted his hat slightly, nodded curtly, and stepped out onto the platform.

Leaning forward to watch this curious man, I trod on something. It turned out to be a cigar case, made of dark morocco leather, with John Derry's initials on the side in a silver monogram. I sprang out of the carriage and accosted the guard, who happened to be there.

"When do we depart?"

"Two minutes, sir."

I dashed along the platform as fast as my legs could carry me. I could see him distinctly, he was about halfway along the platform. As I got nearer, I saw that he had stopped to talk to someone in the middle of a crowd of people.

There was a gaslight quite close to them which, as I quickly threaded my way through the crowd, clearly illuminated their faces. Mr. Derry, with a dubious expression, was listening to his companion. This man was considerably younger and shorter than he was, with a red face and sandy hair, wearing a grey suit.

"Mr. Derry!"

He wheeled around at my shout and gazed at me with watery eyes. At the same instant, I somehow collided with a burly porter who was coming the other way. We bounced off each other. My eyes were turned away from Mr. Derry for a second at the most, perhaps only half a second. But in that time he and the other man had... had gone.

I looked around me, stupefied. It was impossible that the two men could have disappeared so quickly, but they were nowhere to be seen. Had they vanished into thin air? Had the platform swallowed them up. Where *were* they?

"Are you all right, sir?" said the porter I'd bumped into. "You look

I dashed along the platform as fast as my legs could carry me

a little dazed."

"There were two men standing here, just moments ago," I said. "Did you see them?"

"Can't say I did, sir."

A long blast from the train's whistle indicated that it was about to depart. I saw the guard standing outside my carriage door, waving at me frantically. I glanced around one last time, then set off as fast as the crowd would allow. I reached my carriage just as the train was pulling slowly out of the station, and was bundled through the door by the guard. Then, breathless and bewildered, still holding John Derry's cigar case in my hand, I flopped onto the seat.

It was the strangest thing I had ever encountered. One moment they were there, talking, with the gaslight shining on their faces, and the next moment – they were gone. Where? How? I just couldn't stop thinking about it, and the event was still spinning through my brain when I was met by my friends at Dumbleton.

"Hope you don't mind," Jonathan said, "but we've got some dinner guests. Dry old sticks, I'm afraid. Half a dozen of 'em. Decided to do the lot in one fell swoop, then we don't have to see them again until Easter."

I won't describe the guests or the dinner in great detail. There was a country baronet and a country baroness; there was a parson; there was a governess; there was a turkey, and a haunch of venison; and there was conversation, of sorts. To the left of me two ladies discussed their dogs, while to the right of me two gentlemen discussed their horses. It was dreadfully dull, and indeed, became so excruciating that eventually the conversation petered out entirely.

Jonathan, wearing a fixed smile on his face, stared earnestly into his wine glass. Isobel looked as though she was trying to think of something to say, though with little hope of success. Someone coughed. Prompted by this awkward pause, I made the unhappy mistake of telling part of my story.

"By the way, Isobel, today I met a relation of yours on the train."

"Indeed?" she said, looking at me gratefully. "Who was it?"

"Your cousin, John Derry. He told me to wish you a very merry Christmas."

Isobel looked at me, utterly startled, as though I were crazy. Jonathan put down his wine glass rather too heavily, so that some of it sloshed onto the tablecloth. I had no idea why my words had provoked this reaction, so I pressed on with Mr. Derry's joke.

"And he asked me to tell you," I continued desperately, "not to burn down the blue room when there's someone staying in it!"

Before I reached the end of my sentence, I became aware that the other guests were looking at me almost *ominously.* Absolute silence greeted my anecdote. I felt as though I had said something which, unknown to me, was unforgivable for some reason. I sat there, miserable and embarrassed, not daring to say another word, until the parson, a decent and kind-hearted man called Prendergast, rescued me.

"You've been abroad for some time haven't you, Mr. Langford? In Poland, and, and the Baltic, isn't it? You must have had many interesting experiences over there."

I felt very grateful to him, and we began a rather lame conversation which, after a few minutes, thawed the awkward atmosphere a little. Nevertheless, I was relieved when dinner was over. The ladies retired to the drawing room straight away, while the gentlemen stayed behind.

"What on earth did I do wrong?" I whispered to the parson as the servants cleared the table.

"You embarrassed Isobel, in front of the cream of local society, by talking about John Derry."

"What's wrong with mentioning John Derry? He's her cousin."

"*I'll tell you what's wrong with it,*" he replied, dropping his voice to a barely audible whisper. "*Three months ago John Derry took seventy-five thousand pounds of company money and disappeared.*"

"I don't suppose you mistook him for someone else?" Isobel said later when the guests had gone, and I had apologized profusely for my blunder.

"Impossible."

"The fact that he talked about the fire in the blue room," Jonathan said, "proves that it was him. There was a bird's nest in the chimney, you see, so the room was smoked out. How did he look?"

"Absolutely awful, as a matter of fact. Rather odd. Wouldn't shake my hand. Nothing wrong with his powers of speech though," I added ruefully. "That's what makes me think he's innocent. He didn't show a trace of guilt, not even when the guard came around."

"Are you *sure* it was him, William?"

Rather annoyed by this, I went to my room to get the cigar case.

"Oh," she said sadly when I handed it to her. "This is definitely his, he's had it for years and years. It's got his initials on it, in that funny design."

"What a mystery," Jonathan sighed, shaking his head. "I think you and I should go to Blackwater tomorrow, William, and try to sort this out."

"Until a few months ago," the stationmaster at Blackwater told us, "Mr. Derry was a regular visitor here because of the new branch line. But then, gentlemen, I'm sorry to say there was a bit of a scandal."

"So you haven't seen him here recently? Yesterday, for example?"

"Good heavens, no, this is the last place he'd think of showing himself. Everyone here knows what he looks like and what he did. He'd be arrested on sight!"

"My friend came down from London yesterday on the four-fifteen express, and he saw Mr. Derry on the train."

"With the greatest respect sir," said the stationmaster, "I find that very difficult to believe."

"Perhaps you can ask the guard on that train," I replied. "Big fellow with bushy whiskers. He saw him too. Do you know the man I mean?"

"Benjamin Somers. As honest a man as I ever met. He's here now, as luck would have it, waiting to board the eleven-forty."

The man was sent for, and I recognized him at once.

"Somers," the stationmaster started, "do you know what Mr. John Derry looks like?"

"The dirty dog who robbed all that money, sir?"

"Yes."

"Know him anywhere, sir."

"Was he on the four-fifteen express yesterday?"

"The four-fifteen? Yesterday? No sir."

"But you must have seen him!" I exclaimed. "He was sitting in the same carriage as me!"

"I'm sorry, sir, but I haven't laid eyes on him for months," the guard said emphatically, "and if I had, I would've arrested the filthy robber myself."

"Well, gentlemen, sorry we can't be of any help," said the stationmaster. "I think I can safely say that Mr. Derry wasn't on the four-fifteen express yesterday. Now, if you don't mind, I've got work to do."

"But—" I cried.

"Good day to you," was his curt reply.

We were left standing on the platform, watching the retreating backs of the stationmaster and the guard. For some moments we were silent.

"Now look here," Jonathan said suddenly, "are you all right? Bit under the weather from all that travel, maybe?"

"Of course I'm all right!" I responded. "You'll be telling me I dreamed it all next!"

"It's not beyond the bounds of possibility..."

"And this is a dream as well, I suppose?" I said angrily, waving the cigar case under his nose.

I was infuriated by the episode at Blackwater station, and wanted the mystery cleared up. I wrote to the chairman of the East Anglian Line, telling him roughly what had happened, and received a request from him to attend an interview at which Benjamin Somers would be present. I assumed the purpose of the interview was to investigate whether the guard was an accomplice to John Derry's crime. I was wrong.

I was shown into the board-room of the company, where nine or ten grave-looking gentlemen, the directors, were seated around a large table. Three clerks sat at a separate desk. The chairman of the board introduced himself and thanked me for coming.

"This is a great puzzle about Mr. John Derry, Mr. Langford."

"Yes indeed."

"You claim to have seen him on the four-fifteen express from London to Crampton, on, er..." He looked down at a piece of paper; "on the the fourth of December. Is that correct?"

"That's right. He left his cigar case behind. Here it is."

The chairman turned it over in his hands before passing it to the other directors.

"This is quite extraordinary,"

he muttered to himself. "Did you talk to Mr. Derry?"

"Yes, or rather, he talked to me. He told me all about the new branch line from Blackwater to Stockbridge – construction costs, legal issues, land purchase. He was carrying seventy-five thousand pounds in cash."

"He claimed to have seventy-five thousand pounds with him?"

"Yes. It was for buying land."

"Are you aware," another board member asked, "that John Derry stole that exact amount of money *more than three months ago?*"

"Yes."

"And yet he didn't seem guilty or unduly concerned?"

"No."

Two of the other board members began whispering to each other.

"Most unlikely," I heard one of them say.

"And as for that cigar case," whispered the other, "he must have got hold of it from somewhere else."

I felt myself flush bright red with indignation – they thought I was lying!

"Mr. Langford, no doubt you're aware that the company has offered a five thousand pound reward for any information pertaining to the whereabouts of Mr. Derry and the seventy-five thousand pounds."

My mouth actually fell open as I realized what he was implying. He thought I was making the whole thing up in order to get the reward!

"I had no idea there was such a reward!" I said furiously, "and I very much resent what you seem to be suggesting!"

"I'm not suggesting anything," came the calm reply. "I merely wanted to establish if you knew about the reward. Mr. Pilkington, send for Somers, please."

While I sat fuming in my chair, a clerk went to get the guard, Benjamin Somers. The two of us exchanged some hostile looks.

"Somers," the chairman began, "this is Mr. Langford, as I think you already know. He has told us that on the fourth of December Mr. John Derry was on the four-fifteen from London to Crampton. In fact they even shared a compartment. Mr. Langford has a cigar case to prove it. *Was* Mr. Derry in the carriage?"

"No sir."

"Why should I believe you, Somers?"

"Begging your pardon sir, but I've worked for this company nigh on thirty years now, and I've always done my best for it."

"Perhaps. Nevertheless, I want you to tell us plainly your side of the story."

"Well, I'm not used to making speeches, sir, but this gentleman—"

"Mr. Langford, Somers."

"Yes sir, Mr. Langford. Well, he came up to me on the platform at London, and he asked for a private compartment."

"A *private* compartment?" said the chairman, his eyebrows rising in surprise.

"Yes sir. So I showed him to a compartment and gave him the key. Told him to lock the door, and leave the key under the seat when he got off at Clayborough."

"Is this true, Mr. Langford?"

"Well, yes, but—"

"Mr. Langford," said another member of the board impatiently, "on the one hand you claim to have shared a compartment with Mr. John Derry, and on the other you claim to have locked yourself into a *private* compartment. Wouldn't you say there was something of a discrepancy there?"

"Yes, but—"

"Carry on, Somers," ordered the chairman with a weary sigh.

"Yes sir. The next time I saw the gentleman was after I'd checked his ticket at Blackwater. He went chasing off down the platform in a most peculiar manner, sir."

I attempted to explain.

"That was when I realized that Mr. Derry had left his cigar case. I was simply returning it to him, and I was running because I didn't want to miss the train."

"And were you successful in finding Mr. Derry?"

"Er, well..."

"Yes or no?"

"Well, yes, I suppose."

"And yet you failed to give him the cigar case."

"I'm afraid it didn't prove... possible."

"Why ever not?"

"Well," I said desperately, "if I can tell you what happened—"

"By all means."

I launched into my peculiar story, explaining how I had had to fight my way through the crowd to get to Mr. Derry and the man who was talking to him.

"He was with someone?" the chairman asked with interest.

"Yes."

"You'd recognize the man?"

"Oh yes. He was small and slight, with sandy hair, quite a red face, wearing a grey suit."

"You must have been quite close to notice all that," observed a member of the board.

"Yes."

"And yet you failed to return the cigar case to Mr. Derry."

"Er... I'm afraid so."

"The question which springs to mind, Mr. Langford," said the chairman bluntly, "is why?"

I looked around the table, almost frantically. How could I expect them to understand what occurred on that day? How could I myself understand it? Maybe Jonathan was right, maybe I *did* dream it...

"Well, I ran up to Mr. Derry and his companion, shouting his name, and he turned around to look at me, and at that instant I bumped into someone, and then, and then..."

"Yes, Mr. Langford?"

"And then, Mr. Derry, he sort of, vanished. Vanished as if into *thin air.*"

The silence which greeted this claim was almost unbearable.

"How far away were you at the time?" someone asked eventually.

"About three yards."

I smiled weakly. Everyone was looking at me as if I were a complete idiot. Somers shook his head sadly, almost in pity.

"I'm afraid this has been a waste of time," the chairman said, shuffling some papers and standing up. "Gentlemen, let us get back to work. Somers, please accept my apologies. As for you, Mr. Langford, consider yourself fortunate that the police are not involved. It is my profound belief that you intended to defraud this company of five thousand pounds."

The injustice of it! And yet, how could what I was claiming be true? Why would a man who had stolen seventy-five thousand pounds from the company reappear three months later on the company's train? And how could that same man disappear into thin air in an instant? I thought I was going mad. I slumped down in my chair, clutching the cigar case to my chest as though desperately clinging to my own sanity.

The members of the board were leaving and various clerks were buzzing around. That's when I saw him. He came into the room with a sheaf of papers in his arms, distributing them to the other clerks. He was a small man, of slight build, with sandy hair, and a red face...

"That's him!" I yelled at the top of my voice.

The room fell silent. The clerk looked at me, apparently baffled, showing no sign of recognition.

"That, sir, is Mr. Raikes, our senior clerk," said the chairman of the board. "Really, Mr. Langford, I think we've heard quite enough of your ludicrous—"

"I don't care if it's the Queen herself!" I exclaimed in excitement. "That's the man who was talking to John Derry!"

At the name 'Derry', Raikes' eyes briefly widened, but that was the only sign of alarm he gave, and only I noticed it.

"I'm sorry, Mr. Langford, but this meeting is now over, and I must insist that you—"

"Please," I implored, "please, you must question him."

"Don't listen to another word from him," one of the directors said, "the man's mad."

Something in my eyes must have made the chairman give me one last chance, against his better judgement.

"Very well, Mr. Langford. What should I ask him?"

"Where were you," I said to Raikes directly, "on the afternoon of the fourth of this month?"

"I was here," Raikes answered, "in the office. Check the ledger if you don't believe me."

"Check it," the chairman told the clerk called Pilkington.

While everyone waited tensely, Pilkington fetched the ledger.

"Ah yes," he said after flicking through it for a minute or so. "On the fourth of December many of us were hard at work on the Carter-Watkins pig iron accounts. I was involved myself, together with Gray, Flower, Morrow, Raikes..."

"Yes," said the chairman, "the Carter-Watkins pig iron accounts. I remember that day distinctly. Well, Mr. Langford, I've had quite enough of this nonsense. Not only do you try to swindle us of five thousand pounds, but you try to ruin a man who is perfectly innocent. Mr. Pilkington, call the police."

While he was saying all this, I had been staring at Raikes, and Raikes had been staring at me. There are some forms of communication that go deeper than words. My eyes were boring into his eyes, saying, *Guilty, you're guilty!* As for his eyes... his eyes were saying, *Yes, I'm guilty, I'm guilty!* He slumped to his knees.

"I can't stand it any more!" he cried. "I was there! I met Mr. Derry on the platform!"

"But, but you were here," stammered Mr. Pilkington. "The Carter-Watkins pig iron accounts, you were *here*."

"Not then," whimpered Raikes, "I don't know about that, I can't explain it. I was there before, on the twenty-fourth of September."

"But that was the day Mr. Derry took the seventy-five thousand pounds to Mallingford," breathed the chairman.

"Yes. I knew he was going, I took the day off. I met him at Blackwater station, pretended it was a coincidence. I told him there was a shortcut to Mallingford. He came with me, and I... it was in a field."

"Raikes," someone whispered, "what are you saying?"

"Oh, the blood, the blood," Raikes wailed. "I didn't mean to kill him! I didn't mean to!"

He collapsed, sobbing, into a pathetic heap, shielding his face from our horrified gaze.

John Derry was murdered on the twenty-fourth of September, 1857. Who – or what – did I meet on the fourth of December? I have had twelve years to think about this question. I believe his anguished spirit was reaching out from beyond the grave, haunting the four-fifteen express until someone, somehow, cleared his name. Who knows how many other passengers

talked with him, who had never met him before, and knew nothing of his circumstances?

But what is even more difficult to understand is that on that day too I saw the ghost of a man who wasn't dead. I saw Raikes on the platform with Derry, and yet, at the same time, the living, breathing, real Raikes was working diligently in London. Is it possible for the living, as well as the dead, to have ghosts?

Raikes is certainly dead now. He was found guilty of murder, sentenced to death, and hanged. Every Christmas, when I visit my old friends Jonathan and Isobel, I can't help shuddering when the train reaches Blackwater, and I always look out of the window in case I see them – the ghosts of a murderer and a murderer's victim.

The Tall Woman

I first heard about The Tall Woman from my friend Carlos. She was his worst nightmare and his deepest fear. And now, as I write, she has become mine.

Carlos was a brilliant young engineer who lived in Madrid. He was engaged to a woman called Joaquina, his childhood sweetheart from Seville, but she died suddenly in 1859. I visited Carlos in Madrid a few weeks after her death. That morning I found him in his office, working quietly with his assistant on the plans for a new tunnel. He looked half-dead from weariness and grief, but seemed very pleased to see me.

We walked to a little café in the square of San Lorenzo, where children were playing around the small stone fountain, and sat down at a table.

"I'm glad you've come," Carlos said solemnly. "There's something I want to talk about, something I have to tell you."

"All right," I replied, gazing at him anxiously.

"There's something going on, Gabriel, that I just don't understand. It's something incredible, and yet true."

On the outside he seemed quite calm and in control. But there was a film of perspiration glistening on his forehead, and a slight edge of panic to his voice. I realized, with a little shudder of shock, that Carlos was scared out of his wits.

"Gabriel, I never told you about a particular phobia of mine. It's so ridiculous and peculiar and, well, embarrassing, I suppose, that I've never told anyone, not even the closest members of my own family. You see, all my life, for as long as I can remember, I've had an irrational fear of, of...

"Yes?"

"I hardly like to say, but I must. I *must*."

Despite his words, he fell into a nervous silence, showing no sign that he was going to continue.

"Spiders? Snakes?" I asked, in an attempt to encourage him. "You can't tell *me* anything about phobias. I'm still utterly terrified of dogs. Do you remember when we were at college, when that Professor used to bring in his loathsome spaniel, and I had to skip all his lectures?"

"I wish it were as *ordinary* as that. You see, the truth is that I'm utterly terrified of, I, you see, I..."

Once more the words trailed off into silence.

"I wonder where these sorts of fears come from?" I continued. "If I see a really large dog off its leash, my heart starts pounding, and I become convinced that it's going to attack me."

"Well," my friend said, "you're lucky to have such an ordinary terror. Mine is... Ever since I've been a small child, nothing has caused me so much fright, so much *dread*, as the sight – or even the thought – of a woman, on her own, at night."

If it wasn't for the fact that Carlos was in deep grieving, I would have burst out laughing. As it was, I just stared at him blankly, waiting for him to explain.

"You know I'm not a coward," he said quickly. "You know about the duels I've fought, for example. But when I'm walking at night, I'd rather come across three blood-thirsty drunken murderers in a dark alley than a woman on her own. I shiver from head to foot, and visions of ghosts and demons seep into my mind. I become so utterly helpless, Gabriel, that I have no choice but to flee until I get home."

I still didn't say anything. I didn't know what to say. What was so frightening about seeing a woman, alone, at night?

"It has happened to me several times, and each time it has had the same effect. Gabriel, you're the first person I've told this to. I don't know what to do."

Clearly embarrassed, he waited for me to respond.

"Are they," I said after a rather desperate pause, "are they very frightening, these women?"

"Well... No, not really. They don't mean me any harm, they're just ordinary women; an old woman scuttling across a street from one house to another, perhaps, or a young woman waiting at her front door for a friend to arrive. They are perfectly normal, harmless women. That is, apart from one. The Tall Woman."

He wiped his brow with a handkerchief, and a slight shudder

I saw her, not more than twenty paces away

swept across his body, though he tried to conceal it.

"Gabriel, three years ago I was walking home one night after a visit to the casino. I'll never forget the date: November the sixteenth. There was a full moon flooding the narrow streets with a silver light. I was just crossing the corner of the Calle los Peligros when, looking ahead, I saw her, not more than twenty paces away."

"The Tall Woman?"

He nodded.

"She was standing all alone, stock-still, much taller than a tall man, a giant of a woman, very old, wearing a long black dress. Her eyes were fixed on me, bold, malignant eyes, glinting like daggers in the night, while her huge, toothless mouth slowly formed itself into a vile, wicked grin."

"Carlos," I said softly, "I can see that your fear is as real as my own fear of dogs, and far, far more intense than anything I've ever experienced; but the truth of the matter is that this woman was probably just a beggar hoping for money, or—"

"She looked like she belonged to an earlier age," he continued, not listening to me, "and she was fanning herself coyly with a fan, as if she were a young woman teasing me. She was horrible. Repulsive. Her skin was a deathly shade of grey, Gabriel, and her hideous expression still grinned like a malevolent gargoyle. I was petrified.

"Normally, if I come across a woman on her own at night, panic takes over and I sprint away in the opposite direction. But this time, with this woman, I couldn't move. I was locked into her gaze. I stood and stared, while a dread I can hardly bear to remember closed over me. She was a witch. She was a devil. She was evil made human. I felt that she was the reason why I had always been scared of seeing a woman on her own at night, she was the embodiment of my fear; my fear made visible."

Carlos no longer seemed aware of my presence. The conversation had become a monologue, sometimes broken and excited, sometimes flat and matter-of-fact. He was rocking to and fro on his chair, with his eyes fixed and unmoving.

"I had to escape from The Tall Woman, but I was too frightened and weak to run. Finally I managed to move. I edged away, down the narrow street, my hands clutching the walls as if I were on a narrow ledge above a precipice. I had gone about ten paces when suddenly an unbearable thought stopped me in my tracks – what if The Tall Woman was following me!

"I didn't dare look behind, but I didn't dare *not* look either. So I stood there, motionless, for a minute or more, my heart pounding. Then my head turned back to look, almost as if someone else had the power to turn it. And what did I see? She was creeping up on me silently!

"I saw the pitiless glare of her rheumy eyes, the deeply wrinkled skin, hanging in folds, and that vile, obscene grin of mockery. I screamed, and somehow the noise broke my trance and enabled me to run. I ran like a hare from a dog, not stopping till I reached my house on the Calle de la Jardines. I collapsed inside, a quivering wreck."

I could easily imagine what he must have looked like, because by now Carlos was shaking, and his voice was trembling with emotion.

"But my troubles were not over, Gabriel," he said, becoming aware of me as his listener once again. "They were only just beginning."

"She was in the house?"

"No, she wasn't in the house. At least, not in the way that you mean. It was four o'clock in the morning, but my servant was waiting up for me. 'Señor,' he said, once I had pulled myself together, 'Señor,

74

Colonel Falcón has been waiting for you since midnight.' "

Carlos sighed, and his eyes brimmed with tears.

"These words filled me with dread. You see, Colonel Falcón was an old family friend from Seville. He wouldn't have visited Madrid unless it was to bring important news, and as my father had been ill for some time... I rushed into the sitting room and Falcón stood up immediately, the look on his face confirming what I already knew. Traumatized by my experience with The Tall Woman, I flung myself into his arms and began to cry. 'Yes, Carlos,' Colonel Falcón said, 'your father has died.' "

My friend had only told me half his story, but he was so agitated that he looked almost crazy, and I was worried he was going to have a fit. It was important for him to calm down, so I decided to leave and come back later.

"But you haven't heard what happened next," he whispered.

"Later, Carlos. I'll come back early this evening."

"You promise?"

"Yes."

I was glad to get away, not only because of my concern for him, but because I wanted time to think about everything he had told me.

Back at my friend's house that evening, I was led by his servant through the rooms to the back door, and out into the courtyard where Carlos was sitting at a table. When I got nearer I saw that he was working on something, a flat piece of wood on which he carved shapes or letters.

"I didn't know you could carve wood," I said.

"It's just a hobby."

"What are you making?"

"Just a little memento."

He put it to one side and turned to his servant.

"Alfredo, bring us a flask of sangria please, and then see that we aren't disturbed."

"Yes, Señor."

We waited in silence until Alfredo had brought the sangria.

"I've been thinking about what I told you earlier," Carlos said.

"So have I."

"You must be wondering why I'm so obsessed with The Tall Woman, when it's only three weeks since Joaquina died."

"No, of course not, it's perfectly natural to have these strange moods when you're in such deep grief. That's why I have a suggestion."

"What is it?"

"Why don't you leave the city for a few months, find a place in the country where you can recuperate? Your mind is still in shock. A proper rest will make you realize that The Tall Woman is just the product of your imagination."

He smiled at me, almost like a father disappointed that his child doesn't understand something.

"Maybe you're right. Perhaps I should take your advice, but everything will become clear when you hear the rest of my story. Then if you still think it is nonsense," he said bluntly, "I will never mention it to anyone again."

"But you'll exhaust yourself, it's not good for you," I protested.

"Gabriel, I *have* to tell someone."

"But—"

"A long time after my father's death," he interrupted, silencing me with his hand, "I saw The Tall Woman again. It was five o'clock in the morning. It wasn't yet light, but there was a faint glimmer in the sky. I was alone in the street, but I was deep in thought and The Tall Woman wasn't on my mind."

At this point Carlos took his handkerchief out of his pocket and wiped his brow. He breathed in deeply, as if to prepare himself to tell me what happened next.

"When I looked up, Gabriel, and saw her there, in front of me, I nearly fainted with shock. She was only inches away! Where she sprang from, I'll never know. Her loathsome eyes were fixed on mine. Her grin was widening, leering, mocking, and she was fanning herself again, as coyly and slyly as before. Without thinking, I attacked her, like a cat backed into a corner attacks a dog! I flung myself on her, seizing her by the neck and dashing her head against the wall, hard, again and again and again, shouting at her, but—"

"What, Carlos?"

"It had no effect on her! She couldn't be hurt. I let go of her, staring down at my hands, repulsed that I had touched her foul skin. 'Do you remember what happened on the sixteenth of June?' she hissed. How could I forget the day my father died and the date I first saw her? I slowly nodded, once, twice, and she howled with glee. 'You'll remember today as well!' she cackled."

Carlos was shaking. I put a hand on his arm and tried to make him calm down, but nothing could stop him from finishing his story.

"I shouted at her, beside myself with rage – 'I hate you, I've always hated you!' – and she replied in a sly, odious whisper that made me shrink back in repulsion, 'Yes, you have known me all your life, and you have always hated me, but I have known you even longer. I knew you before you were born, and I shall know you after you are dead!' 'Who are you?' I shrieked, trembling with fear, and she replied, 'I am *Hell!*' "

Carlos hissed the word with such violence that I shrank back in shock.

"She spat in my face – a vile, stinking, sticky material that clung to me like treacle – before hitching up her skirts and running away without a sound. I slumped down on the pavement, barely conscious, and was found there an hour later by a priest. I didn't tell him what had happened. He thought I was ill, or maybe drunk. He helped me home. And who do you think was waiting for me there, Gabriel?"

"Who?"

"Colonel Falcón. Once again he had come from Seville to bring me bad news. You see, what I'm telling you now happened only three weeks ago. He had come to tell me that Joaquina, my love, was dead."

Carlos sank down in his chair, covering his face with his hands, overcome with grief.

The story had shocked me and appalled me, and I was worried sick about the state of my friend's health, but did I believe him about this Tall Woman, this harbinger of death? No. I believed that *he* believed she was real. I thought that grief had driven him temporarily insane. Indeed, I even thought that perhaps he had always been slightly crazy, because to have such a distinct phobia, from the earliest days of his chldhood, was a sure sign of instability. Of course, I didn't say all this in so many words, but he knew. He could tell. He never mentioned The Tall Woman again, neither to me nor, as far as I am aware, to anyone else.

As I was leaving that evening, he picked up the piece of wood and began working on it again.

"Can I see it when it's finished?" I asked.

"I'm sure you'll see it when it's finished," he answered without looking up.

A few days later I had to go to the province of Albacete to supervise the sinking of a mine shaft. I wrote to Carlos several times, but received no reply. I heard that he was ill, with gastric fever and jaundice. After nearly a year, I received a letter from his sister which shocked me more than I can possibly say, together with an invitation: an invitation to his funeral. He had sunk into a deep depression, and had just wasted away.

The family estate was near a village a few miles from the city of Seville, and the family vault was in the graveyard of Santa Maria. The ten or twelve carriages of the funeral cortège wound their way through the narrow streets of the old town. Hundreds of people followed on foot, servants and estate workers, all wanting to pay their last respects.

I was in one of the last carriages with three other men, one of whom I had studied engineering with but had not seen much of since. We were talking together about our lives, about Carlos, when I happened to

The Tall Woman

glance out of the window at a particular building.

"Look at that," I said to my companion, pointing to a mosque. "That's a Moorish construction, well over four hundred years old, but I bet it's still standing in another four hundred."

He agreed enthusiastically, and then went on to deliver his opinions on Moorish architecture, at great length and in considerable detail. I'd forgotten how boring he was, and though I nodded politely, I wasn't listening, looking outside at the townspeople, most of whom were stopping respectfully as we passed.

The carriage was moving past a small cluster of people when a woman caught my eye. She was behind the others, a head taller than any of them, and I thought that I saw her looking back at me before the carriage had gone past. I settled back in my seat, deep in thought, though vaguely aware that my companion was still speaking.

"...although perhaps your opinion is different, Gabriel. Gabriel?"

"Sorry?"

"I was asking you your opinion."

"Er," I murmured, my mind occupied with what I had just seen.

"So... what do you think?"

"Mm? Oh, I agree with you," I said, trying to shut him up.

Was that her? The Tall Woman? It had all happened so quickly that I couldn't be sure. I shook my head and told myself not to be so stupid, deciding that there must be more than one tall woman in Spain.

The graveyard of Santa Maria was old, crammed with mournful reminders of the deceased: white marble crosses, carved stone saints, alabaster Virgin Marys presiding serenely over the graves of long-dead

people. Each grave, surrounded by low rails of wrought-iron, was neat and well cared for, many of them decorated with fresh flowers.

The pallbearers threaded their way through the various monuments, carrying Carlos to his final resting place beneath the earth. Behind them followed all the mourners, a long column of family and friends headed by his brothers and sisters. There were so many people that it took a while before they were all assembled around the grave in Carlos's family plot.

We watched in silence as the coffin was lowered into the grave. Then, with a shock of recognition and dismay, I saw a flat, circular piece of carved wood fixed to the coffin lid:

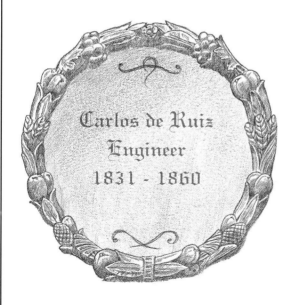

Carlos de Ruiz
Engineer
1831 - 1860

It was the same piece of wood that Carlos had been carving that day in Madrid, when we had sat together in the courtyard. I remembered his words to me, "I'm sure you'll see it when it's finished", and I realized, for the first time, how much I had let him down. He had known he would die unless someone – myself – helped him against The Tall Woman. I didn't.

Carlos's family picked up handfuls of soil to throw into the grave. Following their example, I picked up some soil too, scattering it over the coffin, thinking how I would never see my friend again. I looked up, tears in my eyes.

All the mourners opposite me, dressed in black, were staring sadly into the grave. And standing behind them, head and shoulders above them all, I saw her. My very first glance told me it was The Tall Woman. She was exactly as he had described, with a merciless glare that seemed to bore into my soul, and a hideous, grinning mouth. She was dressed in shabby, old-fashioned clothes, fanning herself in a way I felt I already knew.

We looked at each other across the open grave, she in malicious pleasure, me in absolute disgust. She knew that I was frightened of her, and somehow this made my fear even worse. I managed to look away, surveying the other mourners to see if anyone else was looking at her. None of them were. Perhaps no one could see her but me.

She started to laugh. She closed her fan and pointed at me in mockery, as if she could read my thoughts. At that moment I was wondering if my happiness, my life, my *soul* was in mortal danger – was I going to inherit her appalling curse? I had to lean on the person next to me to prevent myself from collapsing to the ground. Then The Tall Woman opened her fan again, fluttering it in front of her face as she walked away.

At that moment a thought came into my head which reassured me: The Tall Woman was Carlos's demon, not mine. He had been scared of her before he had even seen her or knew what she was, so scared that even the sight of an ordinary woman on her own could terrify him half to death. How could I inherit the curse, when I didn't have that instinctive fear of her in the first place? No, she was here to glory in Carlos's death, but surely she could have no power over me.

As if to confirm this, she moved away between the monuments and tombs, disappearing and reappearing between the many gravestones and crosses, until I glimpsed her for the last time. She had paused by a large marble cross near the entrance to the graveyard, staring at me with her cruel eyes. I shrank back unconsciously. Then she vanished out of sight, and I breathed a great sigh of relief. I was free of her.

The service at the graveside was coming to an end, and some of the mourners were beginning to leave. I bowed my head and said a short prayer for Carlos and then, my mind preoccupied with what I had seen, walked away from the grave.

Shuffling slowly along the path with my hands behind my back, I fell into conversation with a middle-aged woman who introduced herself as Carlos's aunt. As she dabbed at her eyes daintily with a lace handkerchief, I expressed my condolences.

"And how did you know my nephew, Señor?" she asked.

"We first met each other at university, Señora. I'm an engineer, like he was."

"Oh Señor, my nephew was obsessed with engineering! He loved his work, he loved the coming of the railways, with their bridges and tunnels!"

"He was a very fine engineer."

She moved away between the monuments and tombs

Talking quietly in this way, we followed another group of mourners along the path to the gates of the graveyard, where the carriages were waiting to take us to the family home. It was when we came up to the marble cross, where I had last seen The Tall Woman, that it happened: the incident that has haunted me ever since, making every day I live a torment every bit as bad as Carlos endured. The path turned a corner around the cross, and I found myself looking at—

"But Señor, what's the matter? You look like you've seen a ghost – here, take my arm," said Carlos's aunt.

I reached out blindly and grabbed her wrist, holding it so tightly that it must have hurt.

"Are you ill, Señor? Shall I call a doctor? Do you need some water? We must get you to a carriage."

She tried to help me walk, but my legs were paralyzed with fear, and there was no way I could have moved nearer to the dreadful thing in front of us. I pointed at it with a shaking hand.

"Are you scared of dogs?" she asked, laughing. "A grown man like you? Tut tut, Señor..."

She walked over to it, the huge black dog sitting on the path in front of us, that great, slavering hound.

"Shoo!" she cried, raising her walking stick and shaking it, "shoo!"

The beast stood up and loped away. It turned its head back, once, to stare at me again, and that's when I started shrieking, uncontrollably – the merciless glare of The Tall Woman was boring into my eyes. And then, with an almost human arrogance, that vile creature calmly sauntered off among the graves.

The Open Door

After living for many years in India, in 1866 my family came back to Scotland. My wife, Agatha, found us the perfect house to live in, a Georgian mansion. We liked it because it was so secluded, and we were looking forward to a peaceful summer, with nothing more exciting than the odd grouse shoot. Well, we got more than we bargained for – terror, a terror that brought my son close to death.

The name of the house is Brentwood, and it stands on a fine slope of the Pentland Hills, looking out over Edinburgh and the River Forth. There are extensive grounds, and in an overgrown part of them is the ruin of the former house which stood here. It's a desolate and eerie place, in a terrible state of decay, with enormous cedar trees uprooting its foundations, but enough remains to show how impressive the building once was. There's no roof, and the walls that are left are crumbling, but there is the stump of a tower still standing at one corner, and if you hack away at the long grass you sometimes come across some broken pottery or old floor tiles.

One part of the ruin affected me particularly. It was a stone doorway, standing alone with nothing around it but debris and grass. It was arched, quite large, and said to be all that remained of the servants' quarters. Once it would have held a door, a door separating the wilderness outside from the warmth within. Now it was empty and forlorn, standing without purpose. In our first weeks at Brentwood I didn't understand why that open doorway made me feel so uneasy. Just being near it made great waves of melancholy wash over me, no matter how cheerful I might have been only a few minutes before. Later, I was to understand only too well.

Halfway through the summer I had to leave Brentwood for six weeks to do some business in London. While I was there, Agatha's letters made no mention of any trouble with Roland. So I was doubly shocked on returning to my London lodgings one evening, after three days in Kent with an old friend, to find a new letter marked *URGENT* waiting for me, as well as a telegram delivered that very day:

FOR GOD'S SAKE WHY DON'T YOU COME?..ROLAND MUCH WORSE...COME BACK STRAIGHT AWAY...AGATHA

I started packing immediately, and I caught the first available train to Scotland. Every minute of the journey felt like an hour, and I passed it by reading my wife's letter over and over again. She told me that Roland was very sick indeed. The first sign of illness she had noticed, soon after I left, was a particular look in his eyes. Much to my alarm and confusion, she described this look as "haunted".

This haunted look had become more pronounced day by day, and soon Roland was returning from school in the afternoons with his face "as white as a sheet", and sweat "streaming down his cheeks and neck". He refused to tell his mother what was wrong. Eventually she sent for the doctor, Dr. Simson, who confined Roland to his bed. Since then, he had slipped in and out of a dangerous fever.

I arrived in Edinburgh in the failing light of a summer's evening. The carriage I took to Brentwood seemed to creep along the dark country lane, although in reality the horses were almost galloping. I couldn't help thinking that Roland might be dead. When the horses at last thundered up the gravel drive of Brentwood I could see my wife waiting for me at the door. I jumped out of the carriage.

"He is sleeping," she said in a whisper, and I briefly closed my eyes in relief.

Sitting with Agatha in the room next to Roland's bedroom, I learned more about his illness. What I heard worried me more than I can describe. Roland was insisting to Dr. Simson that he wasn't really ill, it was just that he was so scared of something that it was *making* him ill.

"What is it he's scared of?" I asked her.

"A voice, a voice in the ruins, unearthly and in distress. He says it comes from nowhere, that it *doesn't have a body!*"

Of course, this had made Simson even more convinced that the child was seriously ill. I asked Agatha what the voice was supposed to say. My wife's eyes filled with tears, and she shook her head, as though it were too painful for her to tell me. At that moment I heard Roland call out in such terror that I jumped to my feet in alarm.

"Oh, mother, let me in! Mother, mother, let me in!"

"What does he mean?" I asked her in a horrified whisper. "What does he mean, 'Let me in?' "

But Agatha was so upset that she couldn't answer.

I went to my son, who was sitting up in bed, shivering and sweating, holding the bedclothes up to his chin. His hair was damp and lank, and his eyes were like a frightened rabbit's. The nightmare, if that's what it was, had traumatized him. He turned his face slowly to mine and, realizing it was me, managed to smile.

"Papa, you're here."

I sat down on the edge of the bed and held his hand, feeling his pulse pounding fast and furious under the skin.

"Oh Papa, the doctor doesn't understand anything at all!" he panted excitedly, "he makes me stay in bed all day, he – I – there's nothing wrong with me really, Papa! You've got to tell him!"

"We can talk about it later on, Roland," I murmured, wanting to calm him down, but he was too worked up to listen to me, and in the end I didn't have a choice but to hear him out.

"Papa, I'm not sick, it's just that I can hear someone in the grounds who is suffering, horribly, and his voice calls out to me, but when I look there's no one there! I can't stand it!"

His eyes shone so wildly, his face was so white, that my heart sank. He looked half-crazed.

"And what does the voice say,

...shivering and sweating, holding the bedclothes up to his chin..."

Roland?" I asked, although I was fairly sure that I knew already.

He raised himself up from the bed and put his face close to mine, looking straight into my eyes as he *shrieked* the words at me with so much intensity that I shuddered.

"Oh, mother, let me in! Let me in, mother, let me in!"

Was it an hallucination? Was it an extreme fever? Was it insanity? I couldn't tell. I thought it was wisest to pretend to believe him.

"This is very disturbing, Roland. Something has to be done about it."

"I knew that *you* would take me seriously, father. That doctor doesn't believe me, but you do, don't you?"

"I certainly believe that something has frightened you very much indeed. Perhaps there was a lost child out there," I suggested.

My son suddenly grabbed my shoulder, clutching it hard with his thin hand.

"But what if it isn't a living person?" he whispered. "What if it's a ghost?"

My spirits sank even lower, if that was possible. It's unbearable to see someone you love so much in such a hysterical state.

"Papa, promise me that you'll help it! Promise me! It's in terrible, terrible trouble! It's out there, all by itself, just, just *suffering!* I can't stand it!"

He burst into tears, and I heard myself promising, pledging, *vowing* to help the... ghost. Once I had done this his crying petered out, and soon he was quite calm, and almost cheerful.

"I knew you would know what to do," he said.

He fell asleep, exhausted by his outburst.

I was the most perplexed man in the country. The health of my son depended on my being able to help a ghost. Even if I assumed the ghost existed, which I didn't, how was I supposed to help it? What was I supposed to do?

I decided to visit the ruins straight away, and I took my butler, Bagley. Bagley was a large, imposing man who had been in my service, in one way or another, for more than fifteen years. In India he had been a soldier with me, where he had looked death in the face on a number of occasions. He was one of the most reliable people I had ever met.

I told him to get a lamp, and we set off. It was quite dark, but as we arrived at the ruin I decided to extinguish the light. I didn't really expect to find any-one, but if there *was* some sort of intruder scaring the wits out of my

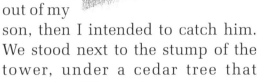

son, then I intended to catch him. We stood next to the stump of the tower, under a cedar tree that seemed to fill the sky.

"Bagley," I whispered, "if you see anyone, or hear anyone, then be ready to seize him."

"Yes sir."

We made our way through the crumbling building. The darkness was unsettling, and the faint breath of wind that disturbed the air had an eerie quality to it. The ruin was certainly a very gloomy place at night, and I felt horribly reluctant to be there at all. If I had been on my own, I probably would have gone home, and come back in the morning. But Bagley was a good man to have with you in a tricky situation, calm and imperturbable.

I suddenly crashed into something, and I couldn't help uttering a little cry of surprise. I reached out with my hands, and found that I had bumped into the old doorway. That same sensation of melancholy which I always felt in that place swept over me. And then, without warning, I heard it.

The blood chilled in my veins. A shiver stole along my spine. Close by us, at our feet, there was a sigh. Not a groaning, not a moaning, not anything as definite as that. It was just a sigh, but it was more horrible to hear than anyone can imagine. I sprang back like a terrified animal, then heard it a second time, a long, soft sigh, emptying an inexpressible burden of sadness into the still and lonely night.

It had a chilling effect, like something cold creeping over me, up into my hair, and down to my feet. The terror intensified when the sigh changed into a wailing full of human misery and pain, that made the blood curdle. My hands shook, but I managed to light my lantern. We were inside what would have been the servants' quarters, had anything remained of them except for the doorway. And it was from the doorway that the sound came.

I saw Bagley – he was lying on the ground with his hands over his ears. He was crying. The sight was so shocking that I dropped the lamp and it went out, so I had to scrabble around on my hands and knees in the doorway to find it. I was exactly where the sound was coming from. It was crying and crying, as though pleading for life, or something even more important than life. Then the words began, and I shook with terror. *"Oh, mother, mother! Let me in! Let me in, mother, let me in!"*

It was unbearable, that call, that plea, there in the empty doorway of the ruin. It went on and on. No wonder Roland had gone wild with pity and fear! At last the words died away, to be replaced by broken sobs and moaning.

"In the name of God," I shouted, still on my knees in the doorway, "who are you?"

I was startled by a large black shape staggering over to me. It was Bagley.

"Come in!" he shrieked. "For pity's sake, whatever you are, be done with it and enter!"

He stumbled over me and fell. I half caught him, and lowered him to the ground. The voice died down. I swear that it seemed to move away, leaving the cottage and going away into the gardens and the night. For some minutes I just lay there, more or less on top of Bagley, recovering my courage. Then I groped around for my lamp. When I lit it, and looked at Bagley's face, I could see that the man was half-crazed with shock.

I had some brandy with me, which revived him a little. It was an alarming and amazing sight to see this once brave soldier reduced to such a pathetic state. I helped him back to the house, where I told some of the other servants to put him to bed. Then I went to the library and sat alone. It had been a terrible night. I had no idea what to do. I had no idea what to say to Roland.

"You've got an epidemic in your house, Mortimer," said Dr. Simson the next day. He called in every morning to see Roland. "First your son, and now your butler raving about a voice, not to mention all the other servants in a flap – and if I'm not mistaken, it's starting to infect you as well!"

Simson was a very rational man, who thought that every effect had a cause, and who pinned all his faith in science. I didn't enjoy being mocked by him.

"Well, as you can't put us all to bed," I told him, "maybe you should suspend your disbelief for a few minutes and listen to what happened last night."

He shrugged his shoulders, but listened to my story in silence. I told him the truth, but at the end of it he was entirely unconvinced.

"My dear fellow!" he exclaimed, in such a condescending way that it made my blood boil. "My dear fellow, I've heard the same story from your boy! And no doubt your butler, when he recovers enough sanity to string a sentence together, will tell me the same! As I said, it's an epidemic! Whenever one person falls victim to this sort of delusion, you can guarantee that another will follow soon after!"

"All right then," I answered, trying to remain calm, "let's assume that it is a delusion. How do you account for it?"

"Any number of things. It might be a trick of the wind or an echo, or perhaps it's an acoustic disturbance, or a—"

"Come with me tonight and judge for yourself."

Dr. Simson laughed loudly.

"And become known as the ghost-hunting doctor? It would ruin my reputation!"

"Well there you have it," I taunted him. "You use the language of the scientist to mock the notion, yet you refuse even to examine the evidence! Do you call that science?"

"Very well," he said after a moment, in the measured tones of a man who is hiding his irritation. "But I'm warning you now, I'll *prove* that this is all nonsense."

"Nothing would please me more," I told him.

We arranged to meet shortly before midnight, and Dr. Simson went on his way, extremely annoyed with me.

"I suppose you'll be having priests and bishops crawling all over the place next," was his parting shot, "holding up crucifixes, exorcizing devils, denouncing demons! It's all stuff and nonsense, Mortimer! Stuff and nonsense!"

I managed to laugh, but in fact Simson's taunt was quite prophetic. When I told my wife about what had happened on the previous evening, her first words to me were:

"We have to get a minister, a man of God!"

I must admit that my opinion on this point was similar to Simson's. I was very reluctant to see some priest roaming around my grounds, swinging an incense burner over my rhododendrons while intoning antique Latin chants. Agatha, however, was adamant. She told me to contact a minister called Dr. Moncrieff, a very old man, long retired, who lived by himself in a secluded cottage a few miles away.

"*He* will know what to do," said my wife trustingly, much like Roland had thought *I* would know what to do.

"Perhaps that's your dreaded voice, Mortimer!" Simson laughed, clapping me on the back heartily as an owl hooted.

We were standing by the door-way with Dr. Moncrieff. A thin moon was peeping from the clouds above, and occasionally I saw bats wheel across its sliver of light. Simson was entirely unaffected by the mournful mood of the place, telling jokes and keeping up a cheery stream of banter. I didn't find Simson's jokes funny, but then, only I knew what we were waiting for, and how dreadful it was.

Simson had been absolutely disgusted when I had arrived with the minister. If Dr. Moncrieff sensed Simson's hostility, he didn't show it. In fact Dr. Moncrieff had barely uttered two words all evening. When I had gone to see him earlier in the day he had listened carefully to my story, sighed heavily, and said, "Maybe the Lord will provide a way, Colonel Mortimer."

Only I knew what we were waiting for, and how dreadful it was

Now, the three of us waited for the ghost. The scene was well-lit, because all of us had brought a lamp or lantern. We had been waiting for over an hour, a fact which Simson reminded me of all too often.

"It's always the same," he said, shaking his head. "Ghosts, spirits, seances, mediums... A doubter's presence soon proves that the supernatural doesn't exist. I'm surprised at you, Mortimer, very surprised indeed. The only thing we're likely to hear tonight is..."

He continued in this vein while I stood silent, staring out into the blackness beyond the light. I was intensely disappointed and, yes, embarrassed.

"Mysterious manifestations do not seem to enjoy my company," Simson said, thoroughly relishing his victory. "Why do you think that is, Mortimer? Mm?"

He chuckled to himself, then lit a cigar. I was completely furious with him for being so dismissive. Whatever he personally thought about the existence of the ghost, the fact was that some unexplained presence had brought my son to death's door.

"No," he concluded to himself, sighing, "I'm not popular with our supernatural friends, but we shall stay here for as long as you like. Never let it be said that Doctor Andrew Simson did not give the apparition every chance. You won't hear any complaints from me, Mortimer. Not a word. Not a peep." He paused. "But when you *do* think we've been standing here in the chilly night for quite long enough, let me know, won't you? There's a good chap."

I was livid, and I would have replied very rudely indeed if, at the very moment that Simson stopped speaking, there had not been an eerie moaning noise.

"Don't play silly games, Mortimer," Simson said in an angry voice.

"I can assure you that I'm not," I answered, with equal hostility. "How could I make a noise like that? It sounds as if it's some distance away."

"It's probably that blasted minister of yours."

The haunting sound appeared to be approaching us from some distance away in the grounds. We listened intently. The sound changed to little pants and fierce sobs, getting nearer and nearer, as though a person in distress were walking to where we were.

"There's a child out there!" Simson whispered urgently. "What's a child doing out so late."

I remained silent. I knew that it wasn't a child, not a living one anyway. Simson moved into the empty doorway and held out his lamp.

"We'll soon see who it is. There's nothing like a good dose of light to flush out a ghost!"

But the light only illuminated what we could see already: the walls all around us, crumbling; the trunks of the cedar trees disappearing into the darkness, and the faint track that led up to the open doorway.

Now the voice was only inches away. It started on a mournful whimpering that made Simson sink to his knees.

"What in the world is it?" he called to me just as it began to howl and shriek with a piercing, unbearable grief.

Simson's body – I say his body, because it seems the most accurate way to describe how he reacted – Simson's body went into a spasm of shock, his limbs twitching horribly, his head thrashing on his shoulders, before the voice wailed the plea which I felt I had already heard a thousand times, a plea which had to be answered if Roland was to get better.

"Oh mother... oh mother, mother, let me in, mother! Let me in, let me in!"

I grabbed Simson and pulled him away from the open doorway. The spasm had passed. He stared at me incredulously, holding onto my hand like a terrified three-year-old child, before staring back at the open door, trying to see the thing which couldn't be seen, the voice that had no body.

It was then that I heard Dr. Moncrieff calling out to the voice in an amazed, echoing cry.

"William! William! Oh, God preserve us William! Is that really ye'self?"

These simple words dismayed me. I thought that the old man had become deranged, like Bagley, and gone mad with terror. I abandoned Simson and rushed across to the minister. His large lantern was placed by his feet, illuminating his figure in the strangest way.

"Are you all right?" I shouted, seizing him by the arms.

He didn't answer, shaking me off roughly so he could concentrate on the voice.

His face was paler than I thought a human face could be. He held out his hands in front of him, and although they were trembling, I was suddenly struck with the absolute certainty that he was not afraid. Meanwhile, the voice had altered into a wretched sobbing that caused feelings of grief and despair to take me over. Dr. Moncrieff called out again.

"Why d'ye come here, William, frightening these strangers with your wailing? Your mother isnae here, lad! She cannae let you in! William, cease haunting her poor ruined door!"

The sobbing of the voice grew louder and, if possible, even more insistent. The minister closed his eyes and stayed silent for a moment, as though drawing on inner reserves of strength.

"Away home, ye wandering spirit!" he suddenly commanded in powerful, ringing tones. "Away home! Your mother is with the Lord William. He'll let you in, though it's late. D'ye hear?"

He sank to his knees. I, too, found myself on my knees. The sobbing of the voice started to fade away from us.

"Lord," the minister cried into the night, "take this lost soul into thy heavenly habitations! Fix him fast within thy everlasting love!"

At the exact instant when the minister said "love", and without consciously deciding on the action,

I sprang forward, launching myself toward the open doorway to catch something which I thought had made a violent movement. There was nothing there, but the illusion was so strong that I crashed into the doorway, banging my head and shoulder on the rough stone. Later, much later, when I was able to reflect on this peculiar event, I concluded that I had somehow *felt* – that is the only word which begins to describe it – *felt* the passing of a soul from one place to another.

I lay on the ground, half-dazed for a moment, before Simson helped me up. He was trembling and cold, his mouth hanging open, his speech broken and inarticulate.

"It's, it's gone!" he whispered.

We both looked at the minister, still on his knees, the light shining around his long white hair like a

halo, his arms outstretched to the unseen heavens above. A strange and solemn stillness settled on us. The minister was not aware of our presence. I will never know how long Simson and I stood watching him, like awed sentinels. But at last he rose from his knees, gave a heavy sigh, picked up his lantern, and turned away.

He began to walk to his small stone cottage a mile away over the hill. We fell in step behind him and escorted him in silence to his door. The sky was clearer than it had been for many nights, shining high over the trees with here and there a star faintly gleaming. The air had a soft, serene quality to it. Nature seemed to be at peace with herself again. I thought of Roland, and smiled.

I visited Dr. Moncrieff a few days later. He listened to my eager expressions of gratitude politely enough, and seemed pleased to hear that Roland looked like he would make a full recovery. But at first he appeared reluctant to talk about the amazing events at the open door, and, not wanting to press him, I soon decided that it was time to go home.

"Well now, Colonel Mortimer, I suppose ye'll be wanting to hear about William," he suddenly said as I put my coat on.

I nodded.

"He lived in these parts. He was a very young man when *I* was a very young man," Dr. Moncrieff said, smiling, "which will tell ye how long ago it was. But he was weak, that one, selfish and feckless, the bane of his mother's life, forever causing her heartache and trouble. Then one day – ach, such a long time ago it was – one day, he left his poor wee mother to fend for herself. The high and mighty folk in the old house were long gone – the place was tumbling down even then – and only William's mother, who was a servant of theirs, remained. And William went away. Where he got to, none knows."

The old man sighed and shook his head.

"It was twenty years afore he returned. Twenty years! And he was rich, Colonel Mortimer, rich, and every pound and penny of it earned by his own industry, for he was a changed man from the wild thing of his youth. Only, he had put off his return to his homeland, year on year, until it was too late. His poor mother had broken under the weight of her poverty. She passed away just two days before William himself came back. It was a tragedy. There was such a terrible scene," he sighed.

"I had just moved to these parts as a newly-ordained minster, and they brought me over to the old house, and there he was, raging with grief, flinging himself at the door and begging to be let in. Ach well. I never thought then that I'd experience the same scene again, and more than sixty years later!"

"What happened to him?" I asked.

"He was never a whole man ever after. He took to drink, Colonel Mortimer, gambled his fortune away, and died."

It's many years now since these events took place. I'm happy to say that Roland has grown up to be a strong, healthy man with a wife and family of his own. They visit us whenever they can.

Agatha and I pass our time well enough. We're getting old ourselves, of course, and do less than we used to. But we go for a walk every day in the warmer months, and if we pass by the old ruin I find myself thinking about William, the tortured soul who cried outside a door that wasn't there, night after night, year after year, with no one to take any notice until Roland passed by.

Agatha never tires of hearing about it, it affects her very strongly, but as for Simson – I'm afraid Simson calls it, "nothing but a lot of mumbo jumbo". He came to Brentwood just the other day to treat a troublesome chest complaint I suffer from now and again, and he actually refused point-blank to admit what we both know happened all those years ago.

"Stuff and nonsense," he said shortly. "It was just the union of certain electrical impulses that, in conjunction with highly unusual atmospheric conditions, resulted in a very rare but entirely natural aural effect. I thought so at the time, and I haven't changed my mind since. It takes more than a breath of wind and a jumped-up witch doctor to make *me* believe in ghosts. Now, open your mouth Mortimer and say 'aaaaah' for me."

"Aaaaah," I said.

The years have given Simson the excuse he needs to deny what happened that night. We are in a new age now, of telephones and electric lights and even horseless carriages, and Simson has welcomed it with open arms. For him, science is the new God, and science is capable of explaining everything. But then, as Roland so aptly pointed out to me when he was just a small boy, Simson doesn't understand anything at all.

The stories in this book have been adapted from original tales by Pedro Antonio de Alarcón,
Amelia Edwards, Theo Gift, Tom Hood, Edith Nesbit, Margaret Oliphant and Barry Pain.

First published in 1996 by Usborne Publishing Ltd, 83-85 Saffron Hill, London EC1N 8RT.
First published in America March 1997. Copyright © 1996 Usborne Publishing Ltd. UE

The name Usborne and the device 🎈 are Trade Marks of Usborne Publishing Ltd.

Printed in Spain.